May Wentworth

Fairy Tales from Gold Lands

May Wentworth

Fairy Tales from Gold Lands

ISBN/EAN: 9783337247157

Printed in Europe, USA, Canada, Australia, Japan

Cover: Foto ©Andreas Hilbeck / pixelio.de

More available books at **www.hansebooks.com**

The Moorish Pearls. p. 31.

FROM

GOLD LANDS.

BY MAY WENTWORTH.

List to these legends quaint and old,
Tales of the marvelous land of gold,
Rich in its mines of shining ore,
Rich in romance and mystic lore;
List to these tales, they come unto thee,
From over the waters—the boundless sea.

NEW YORK:

A. ROMAN & COMPANY, PUBLISHERS.

SAN FRANCISCO:

417 & 419 MONTGOMERY STREET.

1863.

DEDICATION.

PREFACE

As a child, I was fond of stories, and well remember the dearth of the intermediate season, when "Jack the Giant Killer," had ceased to please, and I was yet unprepared to enjoy works written for older and more cultivated minds. Children require stories ingeniously written, with a pleasant tinge of romance about them to fix their attention, and a touch of pathos that goes to the heart, to make them good and happy.

In writing these Christmas Tales, I have earnestly hoped they may serve to while away many a weary hour, which finds its place even in the sunny days of childhood.

The scenes of most of these Tales, will be laid in California, a land full of romance and beauty

It is not strange to hear from the miners of "the early days," tales as marvelous as those of the "Arabian Nights."

Of these "early days" I shall write, and of the

Spaniards, and Mexicans who inhabited the country before the coming of the gold-seekers.

Now as I send away the first volume of the series, I think of the children who will read it, of their sweet, innocent faces, and guileless hearts.

May the blessed Christ, who smiles upon them in this holy Christmas season, never leave them, but dwell in their hearts making them pure and happy forever.

MAY WENTWORTH.

San Francisco, 1867.

TABLE OF CONTENTS.

FAIRY TALES.

SANTA CLAUS AND THE CHRIST-CHILD.

It had been raining all day, and the mist hung so heavily over the bay that the vailed waters tossed their troubled billows in unseen restlessness, like the swelling of an aching heart that the mantle of a fair face covers.

Down Pine Street a hundred rills were rushing, as though each had its special and important mission to perform in advancing the prosperity of the queen city of the Pacific. Men passed along fearlessly, cased in the invulnerable armor of India-rubber coats and glazed caps, and now and then a woman dared to trust her dainty little feet to the mercy of mud and water.

Minnie Bell had been very uneasy all day, for she had been promised the pleasure of a walk on Montgomery Street, and she intended to choose a few rare gifts from all the Christmas treasures that brightened the gay shop-windows.

Minnie had not yet learned the woman's lesson, to smile when the heart aches, and be gentle in disappointment, so tears filled her large blue eyes, and the rosy lips pouted with vexation, as she looked out on the pouring rain. Her mamma was a fair, dashing woman, who loved Montgomery Street as well as Minnie herself; doated upon the theatre, opera, and every thing gay, but, of all things in the world, disliked to be annoyed by the petulance and nonsense of children. She lay all day upon a luxurious couch, reading "Les Miserables," leaving Minnie, poor little *miserable* of the household, to take care of herself, and thus I found her alone in the hall, picking in pieces the flowers of a pretty worsted lamp-mat, the very spirit of discontent and mischief. It takes so little to make a child happy, that I am always sorry to see a shadow upon their young faces at the time when this life should be all sunshine, so I called the little one to me, and taking her upon my lap, told her the story of Santa Claus and the Christ-child.

More than eighteen hundred years ago, one fair bright night, when the moon was casting her floods of silver light upon the mountains and valleys of Judea, it seemed to pause in worshipful wonder over the little village of Bethlehem.

Diamonds sparkled in the dew-drops, and emeralds in the green grass of the

meadows, where the shepherds fed their
flocks by night. The shepherds were
amazed, as the holy light shed its soft bril-
liancy around them, and even the grazing
flocks forgot the dewy grass, as a sweet,
unknown voice, from the viewless air, told
them how that night the fair Christ-child
was born at Bethlehem, and lay cradled in
a manger, with horned oxen feeding near
him. A thousand angel voices joined in
the rich deep melody of praise and gladness, and the first Christmas carol echoed
and re-echoed through the mountains and
valleys of Judea.

Wise men from the East, brought
golden treasure, jewels, and rare perfumes,
as offerings to the pure Christ-child. There
he lay in the arms of his fair virgin
mother, Mary, with all the native beauty
of infancy brightening every feature of his
lovely face, and that rare halo of divinity

about him that even the inspiration of
Raphael and Murillo has but half por-
trayed. These immortal artists had only
the colors of earth to paint the brightness
of heaven. The wise men bowed in ado-
ration before the Christ-child and worshiped him as their temporal king, and
for their rich gifts received blessings, and
went away well pleased to their luxurious
homes. Then came an old man, trembling
with timid humility. He was but a poor
keeper of the flocks upon the mountains,
and brought only the few pale flowers of
winter, as tokens of his devoted homage.

"Sweet mother," said he, kneeling, "I
have nothing but these poor flowers and
the unchanging love of a devoted heart to
lay at the feet of the dear Christ-child;
but, thrice-blessed mother, do not turn
away from this humble offering. I bring
thee all I have." Smiles, like the golden

light of morning, shone upon the face of
the fair Christ-child, and he took the flowers more pleased than with all the rich
treasures of the East, that lay unnoticed
around him.

The holy mother blessed the poor man,
and with a voice teeming with maternal
love and divine richness, she said: " Thy
pure, loving heart is an offering dearer to
the Christ-child than all the riches of the
world, and these flowers are a fitting token
of thy love. Thou shalt not die as other
men do, but thou shalt sleep, to awaken
each Christmas eve, and gladden young
hearts through all time, and in all lands,
with thy welcome Christmas gifts, and the
blessing of the Christ-child shall rest upon
the spirits of childhood through the holy
Christmas season. "

And thus it is that in all countries we
hear of the good Santa Claus, who brings

such beautiful presents on Christmas eve. In the cold north countries he wraps himself in furs, and rides swiftly over the crusted snow in a sleigh drawn by reindeers, his long beard shining with the frost of winter. In the sunny South he rides in a light car decked with flowers.

"But, May," said the now happy Minnie, smiling; "when Santa Claus comes to San Francisco he'd better bring his India-rubber coat and overshoes."

"I've no doubt he will, darling," said I, kissing the little face beaming with earnestness and beauty; "and perhaps he'll bring his umbrella, too, but 'twill make him no Paul Pry—I'm sure he won't intrude."

"No, indeed," said Minnie, "I want to see him too much for that. Do you think, May, if I sit up till ten o'clock, I shall see dear old Santa Claus?"

"I think, little one, if you go to bed at eight and sleep sweetly, he may come to you in your dreams. He generally manages to came when children are sleeping."

Thus it was that little Minnie forgot all her sorrows and disappointments in the anticipated vision of the good Santa Claus. The rain fell heavily, but in the sunny heart of childhood all was happiness.

Now, a "Merry Christmas" to you all— young and old! May the blessing of the pure Christ-child attend you, and Santa Claus be munificent in his beautiful Christmas gifts!

THE MOORISH PEARLS.

MANY years ago, near the Mission of Santa Barbara, there lived a wealthy Spaniard and his wife, who had been married a great many years, and were still childless.

It was the cause of great regret to both, especially to the mother, who loved little ones dearly.

Every day she made an offering to the blessed Virgin, and prayed her to have compassion on her loneliness, and give her a dear little child to take care of, and love.

At last her prayers were answered.

One Christmas eve, when gifts in memory of the blessed Christ-child, were making so many young hearts happy, a beautiful

little daughter was given to her, making
her the happiest, most thankful woman, in
all Santa Barbara.

As the parents were very rich, all the
great Spanish families in the county were
present at the christening; and all the
priests from the Mission of Santa Barbara
were invited.

There was a great feast, and every one
was delighted; but, above all, the father
and mother blessed God for his precious
gift, which they prized more than all their
great riches.

The little girl grew finely, and was very
beautiful, not like the lovely children of
the North, fair and golden haired, but
her complexion was a rich olive, with the
pure crimson blood of health tinging her
cheeks, and her lips were red as ripe
cherries. Her hair, in the sunshine, had a
soft purple hue; in the shadow, it was

black as a raven's wing, and her dark eyes were as soft as a young gazelle's.

She possessed in a wonderful degree, the symmetry and grace of the Spanish women, and her hands and feet were so small and exquisitely formed, that they were the marvel of the whole country.

In the family there was an old duenna, who had taken charge of the mother when she was young, and, to her superintending care, the little one was intrusted.

Years before, the old duenna came from Spain with the mother's family, and her love for the beautiful lady whom she had nursed in infancy, almost amounted to a passion; but for the proud Don Carlos, the husband, she had a jealous hatred, though he was always kind to her, and made her life in the " wilds of the strange country," (thus she always spoke of California,) as pleasant as possible.

Though she called herself a Christian, the
wild blood of the Moors flowing through
her veins, tinged her life with the mysti-
cism and fire of that fated race.

Sometimes she would give herself over
to strange devices and superstitions, which
were very displeasing to her devout mistress, but the old woman covered these
distasteful habits with so much art and
affection, that she enjoyed the confidence
and love of the good lady, and generally
every thing moved on very smoothly and
pleasantly, at the Buenna Vineyard.

The house was large and commodious,
built, like most Spanish houses in California, in the form of a square, with an open
court in the center, and broad piazzas on
all sides. It was very cool and pleasant,
with its latticed windows, and vine-covered
porches.

In the rear was a beautiful garden, surrounded with a high, strong wall, and massive gates with bolts and bars.

There, in a grape-vine covered arbor, the purple fruit hanging within reach, the old duenna loved to sit, spinning lazily with her distaff, now and then stopping to see that no harm came to the little Lenore in her play, and often calling her to her side, to listen to some quaint old Moorish legend.

The father and mother were very fond of their little daughter, and gave her every thing that heart could wish. One day, when the little girl was about ten years old, the father called her to him, and said: "Papa is going away, far across the waters to the fair castellated land, which has been your childhood's dream, to dear, beautiful Spain, and what shall I bring back for my little daughter?"

Lenore's eyes grew large and liquid.

"Beautiful Spain! beautiful Spain!" she exclaimed, clasping her hands in ecstasy.

"Every thing there is so lovely, how can I tell what to ask, dear papa; but wait one moment," and she ran to the garden arbor, and told the duenna all, and said, "What shall I ask?" The old woman frowned till her brows met, then she laughed strangely, and said, "You shall ask for a string of pearls, as pure and white as snow, and as large and clear as the dew drops."

Lenore ran into the house, and throwing her arms around the father's neck, ran her pretty fingers through his hair, and said, "I would like, papa, a string of pearls for my hair, as pure and white as snow, and as large and clear as dew-drops in the first flush of the dawning."

The father looked at the little lady with a heart full of love and pride, and he kissed fondly the little, pure, oval face that was lifted to his, and said, "My little daughter shall have her wish, let it cost what it may."

The little girl clapped her hands, dancing about the room, full of happiness, saying, "The dear papa! the dear papa will bring me the most beautiful pearls in the world."

Her childish joy was subdued when she looked at the mother, who had a smile of love on her lips, but a tear of sorrow in her eyes.

Then the father said, "What shall I bring mamma?"

The mother answered, laying her head upon his shoulder, "Only yourself, dear husband, and your precious love." A tear came to his eye, but he brushed it hastily away, and whispered, "I shall soon return, dear wife, to my dearest treasures;"

then he kissed them both, tenderly, and went away, leaving Lenore and the mother weeping bitterly.

Lenore soon sobbed herself to sleep, with the tears resting upon her eyelashes and cheeks. The sunlight stealing in, and shining full upon her innocent face, made a tiny rainbow over her head.

The sad mother saw it, and thanked God that the bow of promise overbends its beautiful arch over all childish griefs, and she wiped away her own tears, saying, " He will return again, my dear husband, why should I distrust kind Heaven."

When Lenore awoke, her pretty face was wreathed with smiles, and, kissing her mamma, she ran out into the garden to seek the old duenna.

She found her in her favorite arbor, spinning, but when she saw Lenore she laid aside her distaff, and drew the child to her, with a mischievous smile upon her dark face.

Her treatment of Lenore had always been marked by a strange commingling of the love she bore the mother, and aversion she felt for the father, but through it all, she wove a web of fascination, that gave her great power over the susceptible heart of the young girl. Lenore sat down by her side, and for a while she talked of Spain, smoothing the child's hair caressingly with her wrinkled hand, then she told her a curious legend; of how Boabdil, the Moorish king, had once a string of pearls like those she had asked the father for, and how, after the Spaniards had overcome the Moors in a great battle, he intrusted these lustrous gems, with much other treasure, to one of his servants to be hidden upon a distant island, but, by some strange misfortune, as they neared the landing, the Moor dropped the pearls into the sea.

Now this Moor was an enchanter, and, because he could not recover the lost treasure, he cast a spell upon it, that would bring death to the first, who should touch the pearls, perpetual servitude to the second, and riches, honor, beauty, and love to the third, who should retain them in the family forever.

"No matter how many years should elapse, this would surely come to pass," and again the old duenna laughed that strange, unpleasant laugh. Lenore, trembling with fright, sobbed convulsively, "Oh! the dear papa! the dear papa! he will die! I will call mamma, she will send a messenger for him, he shall not touch the horrid pearls," and she started up to go, but the duenna caught her. "Silly child" she said, "I will tell you no more pretty stories, that

was only a legend, and the pearls were not
real and true, but only dream pearls, just
to please my pretty child. " She soothed
Lenore and laughed again, till her tears
were dried, and she joined to the shrill
voice of the weird duenna, the merry,
childish laugh of trusting innocence. The
days of absence passed by in dreamy
quietude at the Buenna Vineyard.

The wife was very lonely, for no one
could supply the place of the loved husband in her heart. The pretty, dark-eyed
Lenore missed the dear papa sadly, but her
time was much occupied by the master
who taught her music, French, and English.
Spanish she learned from the duenna, who
in this language was quite a scholar.

Everywhere she followed the young
Lenore, and, in her varied moods, treated
her with a curious combination of love and
selfishness, tenderness and severity, but,

through all, maintaining her unbounded influence over her charge.

Full of wonderful legends of the Moors of old, she fostered a love of the marvelous in the mind of the maiden, till often she would waken in the darkness of the midnight, from fearful dreams trembling of superstitious dread. One morning early, she ran into her mother's chamber and woke her kissing her eyes and cheek.

"Oh mamma" she said, "do wake up, I have had such a beautiful dream about Boabdil's pearls, pure and white as snow, and large and glistening as the dew-drops. Some one from Spain brought them to me, so noble and handsome, mamma, that I could not help loving him dearly, and I was so happy." "But, Lenore," said the mother, "where was the dear papa." "Oh, mamma," said Lenore, "I did not see him, he was not there."

A strange terror filled her heart, and looked out from her startled eyes, and she buried her head in the pillow and wept piteously.

" 'Twas only a dream, my daughter," said the mother, tenderly, but still Lenore sobbed. " How could I forget the dear papa, for a stranger and a string of pearls." Then the mother kissed her, and soothed her till she was comforted. Soon after a ship arrived, bringing letters from the father. " I am now in Spain," he wrote, my dear, native land. Bright Castile! the world has nothing like thee! No mountains like the snow-capped Sierras, no valleys like Granadas, and no river like the blue Guadalquivir, but, " where the treasure is, there will the heart be also," and my greatest earthly treasures, wife and child, are in California, and, though far away in castellated Spain, my heart wings

its way homeward, and every delight is
treasured, to be renewed again, with you.
I shall soon return to you, dear wife, the
husband you love, but little daughter,
the pearls, 'pure and white as snow, and
large and clear as the dew-drops,' I have
not found in Spain, but have heard of them,
and if possible you shall have them at
any price."

He wrote a long letter, glowing with
hope and affection, promising a speedy return, and the mother took heart again, and
was happy, while Lenore thought with delight, how beautifully the rare, Moorish
pearls would glisten in her purple hair.

She seemed to have forgotten the dream,
and the legend that frightened her so
much. Even the name of pearls chained
her listening ear, and the duenna often
talked of them, their great beauty, and
how pure and lustrous they shone among

the crown jewels of the Moorish king, till
the imagination of Lenore was spell-
bound, by the magic beauty of the won-
drous pearls. Often she would say, "Mamma, show me your pearls."

Then she would take them in her hands
and count them, or twine them round the
bands of her purple hair.

"Beautiful," she would say, as the sunlight kissed them, "but not clear and large
enough. 'Pure and white as snow;' and
large and clear as the dew-drops, these are
not so, but the dear papa will bring them."
Lenore's great gift was music.

She would often sit in the twilight, and
improvise rare snatches of melody, and
when the mother would say, "What is that
Lenore?" she would answer, "My string of
pearls, mamma," and go on playing as
though the genius of music thrilled her
dainty fingers. One day the duenna called

her to an old lumber-room, to see a picture. The picture was really a good one, but had been cast aside because the frame was broken. 'Twas of a fair young girl, standing upon a rocky shore, looking eagerly out upon the waters, at the white sails of a ship the wind was wafting toward her.

"What does the picture represent, Lenore?" said the duenna. "'Tis a maiden watching on the shore, for the ship that brings her dear papa and the Moorish pearls, clear and white as snow, and large and glistening as the dew-drops." The old duenna smiled, as Lenore took the picture to her room, and hung it over her bed where she could see it on waking.

Every day they went to the sea-shore and looked out upon the waters, for the white sails of the ship that was to bring the father, till at last one evening, when all the west was gorgeous with the radiance of golden sunset clouds, the ship seemed to rise out of the waters, and there, on the sanded sea-shore of Santa Barbara, was the living picture of the lumber-room.

The duenna had called Lenore from the garden early, saying, "At sunset the ship will be here; come pretty child, let us hasten to the shore," so Lenore ran and kissed the mother saying, "Mamma! mamma! mamma! the ship, with its white sails spread like the wings of a bird, is flying to us, and I must go. Oh! my snow-white pearls! my beautiful pearls!"

Lenore!" Lenore!" called the duenna, and the maiden ran away dancing, and clapping her hands, as she always did, when very happy. On came the ship till it was moored in the harbor, and with one great rush the passengers came ashore.

Lenore's eyes dilated with delight, but by-and-by an anxious suspense filled them.

"No more! no more!" she cried, "all landed; where is the dear papa?"

The snow-white pearls were forgotten only the father filled her heart.

The duenna cast her eyes around. Don Carlos was not there, and who better than she knew that he could never return.

There was a handsome young stranger in the crowd, and, from his lordly bearing, she knew he must be a hidalgo of the old dominion, so she approached him and asked him for her master, Don Carlos.

"He is not here," said the stranger, "but I bring a rare and beautiful gift for his daughter—the famous Moorish pearls."

Lenore gave one glance at the stranger, she had seen him before in her dreams; and she trembled so that she could not move or speak.

"He is dead," said the duenna.

"He is dead," said the hidalgo, in a low

tone, fixing his piercing eyes upon tho sharp, eager face of the duenna.

Low as the words were spoken, they reached the strained ear of Lenore, and with a wild, broken wail, she fell insensi ble upon the ground.

The stranger handed the box which con tained the pearls to the duenna, and taking the young girl tenderly in his arms, carried her home to the mother.

Poor, heart-broken wife! The pearls had come, but not her treasure. Lost! lost! God, pity all such!

The mother's love was all that saved her from madness; for her child, her beautiful Lenore, she bore the burden of life.

The stranger was kind and gentle.

He told the bitter story as soothingly as possible.

When they arrived at the island, Don Carlos was suddenly taken ill, and just as the ship was about sailing, he breathed his last, first sending his undying love to his devoted wife, and the Moorish pearls to Lenore.

"Tell them," he said, "my last words were to bless them."

In the confusion of the first moments of their grief, the duenna stole from the room, her sallow face flushed with feverish eagerness.

"The pearls," she said, "Don Carlos was the first to touch them, he is dead! This brave hidalgo was the second, and I will be the third to hold this wonderful talisman in my hands."

"Rich, fair, and beloved!

" Can I be fair, so old as I am?

" We shall see!"

She pressed the secret spring, and pure and white as snow, large and glistening as the morning dew-drops, lay the Moorish pearls in their golden casket. She took them in her hand, and held them to the light, and it seemed as though they absorbed whole floods of sunshine. "How beautiful," she exclaimed, then suddenly she dropped them upon her lap, and pressed her hand to her heart.

What a strange, agonizing pain.

It seemed as though chains were riveted about her vitals.

"Can I be the second to touch the pearls, and forever a slave? No! no! It cannot be!

"Don Carlos the first, the hidalgo the second, I am the third.

"Rich, fair, and beloved! But this pain," and again she pressed her hands upon her heart. Slowly she replaced the pearls in the casket, and the pain passed away.

When Lenore recovered she would not look at the pearls.

"Take them away, do not mention the hated gems to me," she said, with a shudder. So the duenna kept them.

Day by day Lenore sat by the dear, sad mother, who only smiled when she looked upon the beautiful face of her child, who grew more lovely with every rising sun, at least so thought the young hidalgo. In their sorrow he never left them.

All that a devoted son could be, he was to the mother, and to Lenore he was every thing.

Very often the duenna sat alone in the garden-arbor, plying her distaff, for Lenore seldom came to her. Often she would steal a glance at the beautiful pearls, saying: "I am surely the third, why am I not rich and fair?"

"Don Carlos is dead, the hidalgo was the second, I must be the third.

"I have the pearls, the rest will follow;"

then the distaff would fall from her hands, and she would dream curious day-dreams, and build castles of her own in air.

One evening, just one year after their deep grief fell upon them, the young hidalgo and Lenore persuaded the mother to walk with them on the beach.

The time had been very long and lonely to her since the sorrow-freighted ship came in, and as she sat upon a moss-covered stone, and saw the white sails of a gallant ship, winging its way to the shore, the tears filled her eyes, and, that her sorrow might not sadden the hopeful young hearts of her children (as she loved to call them), she bowed her head upon her hands, that they might not notice the grief she could not restrain, when suddenly a joyous shout from Lenore sent a warm thrill through her heart, and the blood danced through her veins with renewed life.

"The dear papa," cried Lenore, and sure enough, the proud form of Don Carlos was before them.

One moment and the happy wife was folded to the warm, true heart of her returned husband, and Lenore clung to his arm, weeping for joy.

Once more light and happiness dawned upon the Buenna Vineyard, with the return of the loved husband and father. How beautiful home looked to the wanderer, as he sank into his own chair, upon the vine-covered piazza. His grateful wife sat beside him, and Lenore stood leaning upon his chair.

"How tall you have grown, my daughter," he said, looking proudly upon the young maiden, just blooming into womanhood; "but where are the pearls, my darling?"

"I have never seen them," said Lenore,

"how could I think of pearls and you, dear papa, gone!" And again and again she kissed his bronzed cheek.

"Call the duenna," said the mother, smiling, "we must see the pearls." So Lenore called the duenna from her dreaming in the garden.

"Don Carlos returned! Not dead!" exclaimed the old woman, while her heart stood still with fear, as she entered the room pale as death, and trembling with an unknown dread.

"The pearls," said Don Carlos, after a kind greeting, to which her palsied tongue refused a response.

She gave them to him with a trembling hand, and, as he pressed the secret spring, the golden casket opened, and there lay the wonderful Moorish pearls, pure and white as snow, and large and shining as the dew-drops in the flush of morning.

"Take them, Lenore, daughter," said
the happy father, fondly, and the fair
taper fingers of the maiden clasped the
luminous treasure.

The duenna's eyes were fixed upon her.

How beautiful she grew with pleasure.
Her dark eyes soft as a gazelles, were radiant with light, her red lips parted with
smiles, and the Moorish pearls adding a
new luster to her purple hair.

" Can she be the third?" thought the
duenna, and in a voice husky with emotion
she gasped : " Don Carlos, those pearls !
How came you by them ? What hand has
touched them ?"

"Tell us all, dear papa," said Lenore, not
noticing the duenna's agitation, in her own
delight.

" In all Spain," said the father, " I could
not find the pearls, but I heard of them
from an old Moor.

"He said they were lost near the shore of a distant island, and he promised to procure them for me for a large reward, which I agreed to give him; so we sailed for the island, but I became so ill at sea that when we arrived I was confined to my bed.

"At length the old Moor brought me this beautiful casket, and pressing the spring I saw the pearls, radiant with all their snowy whiteness, but I was so ill I did not take them out, and when I handed them back to the old Moor to place in my cabinet, the pearls fell out into his hands, and flooded the whole room with light. Great Allah! exclaimed the old man, in terror, and, as he replaced them and closed the casket, he fell down and expired instantly.

The physician said he died of heart disease. I grew much worse, and fearing I should die, confided the pearls to the care of our friend, who brought them to you.

and soon after I fell into a swoon so like
death that all thought me dead, and the
ship sailed without me.

"The white sails were not hidden from
sight when I began to recover, but a long,
lingering illness detained me from home,
but thank God I am with you at last, dar-
lings, well and happy."

"And now that my dear papa is home
again, I can enjoy the pearls, the beautiful
pearls," said Lenore, still toying with the
luminous gems.

"More beautiful in your hair than in the
golden casket," said the admiring hidalgo.

"The senorita was the second to touch
them," he continued, "since Boabdil's minion consigned them to their hiding-place."

"No, I was the second, shrieked the
duenna, clasping her hands to her heart,
where the chains of servitude were riveted.

"Always a slave," she moaned, as they

bore her from the room, flushed with the delirium of fever.

For many days she lay prostrate upon a bed of sickness, but when at last she recovered the evil spirit had passed from her forever.

She was kind and gentle, ready to serve any one, but especially the master.

"I am but the servant of servants," she would say. "I will do my duty in the station whereunto I am called. God have mercy upon my soul."

Don Carlos and the mother lived to see Lenore wife of the handsome hidalgo, and the mother of a maiden beautiful as herself, whose purple hair often glowed in the luminous rays of the wonderful Moorish pearls.

"THE TWO GOOD-FOR-NOTHINGS."

A LONG time ago, in a little village on the banks of the Rhine, lived the young boy Karl, in the low, rude cottage of his father, Hans Heidermann, the carpenter.

Karl was the second son in a family of ten children, all boys but the baby in the cradle—the little, blue-eyed Ethel, the pet and darling of the household.

The good Lord had sent to the cottage plenty of children, " the poor man's blessing;" and in their youthful days, when Hans and his good wife were strong and full of hope, the little ones were greeted with smiles of love.

Later in life, when the mother found

that, with all her patient labor, the tiny
feet must go unclad, and eat little as she
possibly could, the supper was not only
poor but very scanty, the boy Julian and
baby Ethel were wept over at their
coming, yet with tears so full of compas-
sionate tenderness that the mother's love
shone through them more sweetly than
through the sunshine of smiles that
dawned upon their first baby.

The youthful days of Karl were passed
in toil, and though the natural joyousness
of childhood would sometimes bubble up
and overflow, the mantle of care fell upon
him very early.

When he was only sixteen, he was quite
a man in his ways, and able to contribute
not a little to the comfort and support of
the family, and he, more than all the rest,
was ever ready to lighten the burden of
the mother's weariness and cares.

When Karl was eighteen years old, he was guilty of a great piece of folly for a poor boy, though I am sure he was not to blame. It was the pretty, violet eyes and sweet voice of the young maiden Chim-lein that made him so much in love with her.

Poor, foolish Karl! with nothing but his handsome boyish face and honest German heart to give her, even his strong willing hands still belonged to the father and mother.

Poor, foolish Karl, to be in love! But he was very hopeful! The brothers were growing strong, and even now all but the little Julian, could add something to the family store. What brightness, wealth, and happiness might not two years bring them all.

One evening, about this time, Karl re-ceived from the merchant, his employer, for

a successful month's work, quite a present
over his usual pay, as a reward for his
faithful industry.

He was very happy as he started homeward, and, looked smilingly upon his
patched clothes, thinking "Now I shall be
able to buy the new suit I need so much,
and I can take Chimlein the beautiful, to
hear the rare music that she loves so well,
and she will store it away in her bird-like
throat, and some day it will gush forth in
loving songs in our own cottage home."
Then he sung gay snatches of his favorite
opera—for even the peasantry of Germany
are born musicians—and, looking at the
sunshine as it danced upon the bright
waters of the Rhine, he blessed the good
Lord for the brightness, beauty, and happiness of life.

Soon the shadow of the cottage fell upon
him, and he entered to find tears dimming

3

the eyes of the mother as she went silently about her work. She wiped them hastily away, but Karl had seen them, and all his bright dreams melted at the sight of the dear, pale face, shadowed by age and sorrow.

Throwing his strong arm round her, he softly said, " What ails thee, mother?"

Then she told him how an old debt of the father's became due on the morrow, and how she feared, she knew not what, because there was no money to pay it.

So Karl put his hand into his bosom and drew forth the treasure that was to bring him so much happiness, and placing it in his mother's hand, said : " Take it, mother, dear ;" and before she could reply, he had gone out into the soft, summer air, down to the banks of the dear Rhine River.

The sun had sunk in clouds of crimson and gold, and the gray twilight cast its cold shadows upon the waters, and Karl's heart had grown very heavy as he thought of the sweet-voiced Chimlein, and her disappointment. "But 'twas for mother," he said. "Poor mother, how pale she looked, her eyes wet with tears."

He walked on, silently, looking with dreamy eyes out of the dim present into the untried future.

One year after, he stood by the mother's new made grave, and, while his heart swelled with sorrow, he blessed God that he had been to his care-burdened mother a loving and dutiful son. And then came the thought of the old clothes that, for her sake, he had worn so long, and he could have kissed the dear old clothes, grown so patched and threadbare, for her sake, the *dear, dead mother.*

After the mother's death, the family was broken up.

The little Ethel and Julian went away
to another part of the country, to live with
a good aunt, who was very kind to them,
and the younger brothers went to trades,
and only Karl and the father remained at
the cottage. Then it was that Karl
brought home the sweet-voiced Chimlein to
be the angel of his house.

"The dear father is lonely," she would
say, as with her quiet words, and small,
white hands she smoothed his pathway
down the rugged vale of dim old age.

The good God only lends us the presence of his angels for a short time, and in
the spring-time he called Chimlein from her
home by the blue Rhine River, to her home
in heaven, the golden, and from the heart of
Karl, her husband, to the bosom of the
blessed Mother.

The cottage was very dark and lonely
after Chimlein went to heaven. Karl went

out to his work with a sad heart, and returned in silence to sit by his desolate hearth-stone, till the fire went out in the midnight darkness.

The father (now an old man with locks white as the driven snow) sat during the long, summer days by the little willow cradle, and sang in the shrill treble of broken and sorrowful old age, to Chimlein's little one; or, when the babe was full of playful innocent life, he would take it down to the banks of the clear Rhine, to revel in the sunshine and listen to the voice of the waters.

To the old man's desolate heart, that child was a priceless· blessing, and in his eyes she was the most beautiful of all the good Lord's fair creation.

When she was three months old, he dressed her in snowy white, and bore her to the baptismal font, where she received

the name of Gretchen, though to the grandfather she was always "schones mein kind"
(my beautiful child).

A circle of golden curls played around
her baby face, and the violet eyes of her
mother shone clearly in the fair light of
the morning, as she looked steadily into
the face of the priest who took her in his
arms and blessed her with the baptismal
water which consecrated her "a child of
God and an heir of heaven."

The old grandfather gazed wonderingly
at the child, as in the softened light of the
sunshine stealing through the cathedral
windows she looked so like the rare picture
of the divine Christ-child.

"She is even now a bird of Paradise,"
whispered tremblingly the old man, as he
received the little one from the priest's
hands. "The angel soul is looking out
from her violet eyes, and heaven's blessed

light falls like a halo of glory upon her
golden curls."

With a shudder, the old man sunk away
into the shadow until the sunshine had
faded from her hair, and rocking her to
and fro, while a master's hand sent rare,
glorious music from the grand cathedral
organ, he watched the violet eyes till they
closed, and the rich brown lashes rested upon her fair baby cheeks. One little soft hand
was tangled in the old man's beard, and
the tone of her gentle breathing told him
that his darling slept the pure, refreshing
sleep of healthful infancy, and once more
his heart was calm and happy.

Karl loved the beautiful child; but
when he looked at her, and saw her
mother's eyes reflected in the dewy light
of hers, a deep sadness filled his heart, and
often he turned quickly away to hide the
glistening of his eyes, and drew his

rough hand over his face to drive back the unshed tears.

"Poor little motherless thing," he would say : "If it was only a boy !" "Poor little daughter, ever too much you will need a mother's care." Then he would snatch up his hat and go out to the banks of the blue Rhine, where the body of the angel Chimlein rested. To the man, nothing is so dear as the pure, true woman of his heart.

Two summers had passed over the head of the little Gretchen, making her more charming than ever, with all the winsome ways of her innocent childhood,

The grandfather was becoming every day more infirm in body, and every day brought his mind nearer to the innocent child who was the darling of his heart. Nearer and nearer to heaven, the golden, he walked with faltering steps through the darkened vale of second childhood.

When at home, Karl would watch sor-
rowfully over these two children, the old
man and the beautiful child; but when he
was away at his work, they were a con-
stant care upon his mind.

In passing his neighbor's door, Karl
often noticed Elizabeth, the thrifty daughter of the house. He saw that her restless
hands were always busy; not one speck of
dust escaped her sharp, black, eye.

Though her voice was loud and shrill
(Karl knew too well he could never find
another sweet-voiced Chimlein) he hoped
her heart was kind, and he thought she
might take better care of the father and
the little Gretchen than he could. So he
asked her to be his child's mother, his
father's daughter, and the mistress of his
cottage.

Elizabeth felt keenly that he was no
ardent lover; but he was her first, and

3*

might be her last; so with no more intense feeling than a desire to secure a home for herself and a provider for her wants, she consented to be his wife, and become mistress of the cottage.

Elizabeth was full of energy, and after she went to the cottage there was a great change in its appearance. Every nook and corner was made thoroughly clean, the rents in the curtains were neatly mended, the bits of carpet were all washed and spread down upon the sanded floor, and there was always a clean shirt for Karl when he came from his work, and a button was never known to be missing.

Altogether there was not a more notable housewife in all the burg than Elizabeth. But her shrill voice grated sharply upon the sensitive ear, and, worse than all, it seems as though the old grandfather and the little Gretchen were always in her way,

From morning till night the old grandfather had a vile pipe in his mouth, and the smoke made every thing black and dirty. She then would look at her clean curtains and whitewashed walls, and frown. He was continually dropping the ashes about, and sometimes would even spit upon the floor, which was too much for mortal woman to bear; and then there was no end to the trouble the little Gretchen made her in a thousand ways.

To think that she, who always disliked children, should be obliged to take care of another woman's child!

At first she would bite her lips and choke down the angry words that strove for utterance, but in her heart she called them "THE TWO GOOD-FOR-NOTHING'S," and would cast such angry looks upon them that in their shrinking sensitiveness they would steal away to the banks of the

blue Rhine and try to forget Elizabeth
and their trouble. But alas! poor unfor-
tunates! too often they would return with
torn or soiled clothes, and then the mistress would be more angry than ever.

It was only for a short time that Elizabeth confined her anger to black looks.
Before she had been in the cottage two
months, her sharp voice would ring its
angry changes upon the *Two Good-for-
Nothings*, as she now loudly called them,
and both the grandfather and little Gretchen went about silent and trembling, like
two culprits who feared detection and pun-
ishment.

She would have them to go to bed
before Karl returned in the evening, for
she was very careful to conceal her unkind
treatment of them from him. He was
obliged to go very early in the morning to
his work, and saw but little of them, and

as the cottage looked clean and cheerful when he returned, he thought they were well cared for.

Sometimes, for whole days the old grandfather and the little one would wander on the banks of the beautiful Rhine River, and in her sweet infantile voice she would rival the songs of the birds.

So wonderful a development of voice in the child was a marvel to all who heard her, and the fond old man's heart swelled with pride as the neighbors gathered round to hear her sing. Every one loved them but the mistress, and they were always sure of a welcome at the noon-day meal from any of the neighbors. The silver-haired old man was "grandfather" to them all, and the little child "mein schonest liebes."

The mistress did not object to their long strolls from home. "The Good-for-Nothings" were only in the way; it did her good to have them out of her sight a few minutes; while they, poor innocents, escaped many a rough scolding, and the little child many a blow from the hard hand of the mistress.

How they enjoyed those days together.

As Gretchen grew older, and the grandfather more feeble, she would lead him by the hand and run to the neighbor's for a coal to light his pipe, saying: "The dear grandfather must smoke." Then they would sit down on the green bank, and with the smoke-wreaths curling above his head the grandfather would tell old legends and fairy tales to half the children in the village, and "little Golden Hair," as the children called her, would sing to them.

One day, when Gretchen was about five years old, they returned from their accus-

tomed stroll to find a new inmate at the
cottage, and Karl called them to look at
the little sister baby. The old grandfather looked sad, for he could not love the
mistress's child as he did Chimlein's, and
he feared it would bring yet greater trouble to his little Gretchen. But the unsus-
pecting child opened her large violet eyes
full of wonder and delight, thinking, as all
little girls do, there is nothing in the world
so pretty as a baby.

But that baby was her destiny.

No more days by the dear Rhine River.
No more songs with the village children,
or fairy tales told under the waving trees
with the fresh air blowing round them.
But the little, golden-haired child became a
fixture by the cradle. The baby would
not go to sleep unless soothed by Gretchen's voice, which now was oftener full of
subdued pathos than childish joyousness.

The grandfather, too, had his hours of
care and watching. But day by day he
was drawing nearer the dark river that
rolled between him and heaven the golden.
His earthly love seemed all centered in
Gretchen. Karl he seldom saw except on
Sundays, and then, in his rough manhood,
though he was always kind to his father,
he seemed a great way off with the harsh
Elizabeth for his wife.

Only Golden Hair, knew and shared the
old man's cares and sorrows. At night
she slept in his bosom and always rested
in his heart.

The two "Good-for-Nothings!"

Alike sufferers from the mistress's harsh-
ness, how they loved each other, though
they dared not show it when the mistress
was near. She was angry at such nonsense, as she termed their holy affection.

The winter after Gretchen was six years

old, was very cold and stormy. The blue
waters of the Rhine had grown black and
sullen. In the cottage times were not
improved. The baby was teething. The
mistress was not well, and visited her accu-
mulating ills upon the poor Good-for-
Nothings.

She would not have allowed Gretchen
to sing at all, but for the baby, of whom
the little girl now had nearly the whole
charge. And very thin and pale she
looked, with the rich flush of her golden
curls falling upon her white forehead, and
her violet eyes large and languid ; but her
little hands were red and hard, poor little
hands that had so much to do.

Child as she was, the woman was grow-
. ing in her heart, and with tenderest care
she watched the grandfather who had no
one but her who understood his sensitive
feebleness, and loved to care for him.

Many times in the day, when the mistress
was out of the room, she would put her
little hand in his, and kiss him. Only the
sick and sorrowful know how sweet was
the pressure of that loving hand.

One day, in that miserable winter, the
baby had been more troublesome than
usual, the mistress more unkind and ex-
acting, and the Two Good-for-Nothings
more silent and depressed. Gretchen had
been whipped because she did not sing;
but how could she, when the grandfather's
chair had been moved to be out of the way,
into a corner far from the fire, and he was
trembling with cold; and, more than this,
Gretchen saw by his heavy eyes and pale
face that he was ill—how much, poor child,
she did not know.

After a time the baby slept, and the
mistress left the room. Then Gretchen
stole to the old man's side, and threw her

arms round his neck, and begged him to
draw near the fire.

"Never mind, Golden Hair," said the
old man, "grandfather is going where
he will never be sick or cold any more.
But, oh, mein kleines kind (my little
child), 'tis thou that break'st my heart.
To leave thee alone! mein liebes, mein
schonest."

Tears gathered in the dim eyes of the
old man, and the cold, withered hand
stroked lovingly the golden hair of the
little maiden, who looked wonderingly at
him with her large, violet eyes glistening,
and the big tears rolling down her pale
face.

"Mein kleines Gretchen, she'll whip
you, and call you *Good-for-Nothing* when
your old grandfather's gone; but sing,
mein liebes, sing all you can; the good
Lord will hear the voice of his own.

Oh ! to leave you, kleina, 'tis so hard ! so hard !" And the old man rocked himself to and fro, weeping and trembling with cold and sickness.

The little Gretchen threw her arms around his neck, kissing his tears, and, half choking with sobs, she whispered: "You'll smoke, grandfather, darling; your little Golden Hair'll get your pipe." Little child! she could think of nothing else, and she must do something for the dear grandfather; and often before, the pipe had been a great solace to him, when the mistress had been unkind; so the little nimble feet ran for it, and brought it to him filled, and with the red coal glowing in the bowl.

Just then the baby cried out, and Elizabeth entered in time for her sharp, black eyes to take in the whole scene.

Snatching the pipe angrily from the little child's hand, she threw it against the chimney, breaking it into many pieces "I'll teach you to leave the baby to be playing with fire. Take that, Good-for-Nothing." And she gave Gretchen a sharp blow upon the little golden-crowned head, and pushed her toward the cradle, adding, "see if you can sing now!"

And Gretchen tried hard to obey, but 'twas a wail, broken with sobs, that rose from the bursting heart of the child, through the winter cold air of the Rhine land, to the feet of the good Lord who took little children in his arms and blessed them.

That night when little Gretchen was sleeping, her weary head resting on the grandfather's bosom, his troubled spirit passed alone and silently through the dim portals of the dusky way, and, entering the pearly gates, found perfect rest in heaven the golden.

In the early morning, Karl was awakened by a wild, piteous cry.

'Twas little Gretchen. The grandfather was cold, icy cold, and she could not warm him, though she had rubbed him till her own little hands were like ice, and had pressed her soft, warm cheek to his.

She could not warm him! He could not speak to her—not one word from the dear grandfather for the poor, little, motherless child, now the lone " Good-for-Nothing."

When Karl found that the grandfather was really dead, with the big tears rolling down his cheek, he took the little Gretchen in his arms, and wrapping a blanket round her, walked to and fro, trying to soothe her.

He loved the old father and the little daughter. But the poor man's lot leaves little time for endearing cares. He must work early and late to procure even coarse food and clothes for his family.

Little Gretchen's bitter, but uncomplaining grief brought tears to the eyes of the kind neighbors, as they looked upon her sad, pale face, and large eyes, so filled with the shrinking loneliness of her sensitive nature. Even the mistress's heart was touched by the hopeless agony of the little one, and while the grandfather lay dead in the house, she was more gentle and kind to her than she had been before.

In a few days they buried him under the trees, by the blue Rhine River. By Chimlein's grave, where he had so often listened to the sweet voice of his little Golden Hair, the poor old " *Good-for-Nothing* " sleeps his last, cold sleep.

Very wearily rolled now the years for Gretchen.

As she grew older, the household drudgery fell upon her. The mistress seldom gave her a pleasant look or word, and no matter what went wrong with the house or children, the burden of all fell upon the poor "Good-for-Nothing."

The mistress had now four children, of whom Gretchen had almost the entire charge; and, at the age of fourteen, in the frail form of a delicate child, she bore the heart of a subdued and sorrowful woman.

She had had no opportunities for improvement, always at work in the cottage; yet her voice, a marvel in infancy, increased wonderfully in strength and clearness. It was a God's gift, and she sung with matchless sweetness and taste, heaven taught.

One day, as Gretchen sat rocking the youngest child in her arms, and singing as only she could, there came a knocking at the door. The mistress opened it, and saw a tall, sweet-faced lady dressed in deep mourning.

There was a fine carriage at the gate,

and she knew by the lordly coat-of-arms, her visitor was no ordinary person, so she dropped a low courtesy and waited.

" Was it you, my good woman, I heard singing just now ?" said the lady.

" Ah, no, madam, 'twas only Gretchen, the Good-for-Nothing, putting the baby to sleep."

" But the Good-for-Nothing can sing beautifully, and I would hear her again."

So the lady entered the cottage, to find Gretchen bending over the now sleeping child, with the flush of shame crimsoning her cheeks, for she had heard Elizabeth's coarse reply. But she rose and courtesied to the lady, and, as she did so, the old broken comb fell from her hair, and a shower of rich golden curls covered her neck and shoulders.

Poor little Gretchen ! How the accident

4

confused her. She did not know that she looked very beautiful, and that her modesty was an inexpressible charm.

"Sing again, my child," said the lady, kindly.

And Gretchen sang a little German song, full of pathos and beauty; and though her voice trembled with agitation, it lost none of its pure richness.

Tears came to the lady's eyes, and, as if speaking to herself, she said :—

"My little Adela was about her age; these golden curls are like hers, and she sang sweetly, but not like this child."

Then the lady drew Gretchen to her, and asked her if she would be her little girl, and love her.

She told her how her own little daughter had died, and Gretchen told her of the dear grandfather; then she threw her little, weary arms around the fair lady's neck, and they wept together—the *childless mother* and the *motherless child.*

Elizabeth was very angry when she found the lady wanted to adopt Gretchen. "The miserable Good-for-Nothing," after all the trouble she had had with her, and just as she was beginning to be able to "earn her salt." And she was to be the rich lady's child, while her own children must remain in poverty. 'Twas too much, and she determined to prevent it.

She went out to meet Karl, and told him her querulous story.

But Karl loved his child, and when the lady told him she would make Gretchen as her own child and love her dearly, he kissed his little daughter, and placing her hand in the good lady's, told her he had never been able to do for Gretchen as his heart desired, and he blessed the good

Lord that she had at last found a friend who would give her a mother's care and love.

So they went away together, the high-born Countess and the beautiful peasant child.

The little Good-for-Nothing grew up to be a lovely and accomplished woman. Her matchless voice became the marvel of the gifted and high-born, as it had once been of the village peasantry.

After she had arrived at a proper age she married the countess's nephew, who had loved her tenderly for years, and lived to see her children's children noble, prosperous, and happy.

In her prosperity, Gretchen did not forget her toil-burdened father, and even Elizabeth and her children shared the favors heaped upon him by the once despised *little Good-for-Nothing*.

In the "early days" a gallant ship left the harbor of Hong Kong, in the land of the Celestials, bound for the port of San Francisco.

Among the emigrants was a young China boy, of the better class, whose father and mother had both died suddenly, leaving to their son only the memory of the happy days of the past, over which a fleeting prosperity and paternal love had cast the halo of perpetual sunshine.

His father was a merchant, supposed to be immensely wealthy, but after the debts of the house were paid Ching Chong found himself alone in the world, and very destitute.

One evening as he walked out through the suburbs of the city, he met a merchant who had been a great friend of his father. The old gentleman stopped the boy, and kindly inquired what he was doing, and how he had been getting along since his father's death.

Ching Chong was feeling very desolate, and at these expressions of interest the unbidden tears began to flow down his cheeks, till, unable to restrain himself, he bowed his face upon his hands, and sobbed as if his heart would break.

The old man gave him time to recover himself; and when the boy dashed the tears proudly away with the back of his hand, trying to call up the dawning manhood in his heart, he said: "I will help you, you are the son of the friend of my youth, you shall be my son."

He took the young Ching Chong by the hand, kindly, led him home to his own house, and provided him with the best instruction the city afforded.

At the age of fifteen, Ching Chong was as handsome and intelligent a boy as could be found in the city of Hong Kong.

One day his benefactor called him to him, and told him of the distant gold land. "There, my son," he said, "you shall go to seek your fortune. I will provide you with every thing necessary for the journey, but you must keep a strict account, and at the end of five years return, and share the gains with me."

"If you do well in all things, I will reward you doubly, for I love you as my own son."

Here the merchant embraced him so tenderly, that the eyes of Ching Chong were moistened with tears of gratitude.

Then the merchant gave him much good advice, which the young Ching Chong promised faithfully to follow.

As the dusk of evening came on, both grew thoughtful and silent; at last the old man took the boy's hand in his, say ing: "I have been thinking of a curious legend which our fathers believed."

Then he told him how years before two Chinamen, a giant and a dwarf, went out into the great world, far beyond the shining waters, to seek their fortune together. How, after a weary time and great labor, they found a cavern full of gold and precious stones, but at the entrance sat two men guarding the treasure.

The Chinamen were very cold and hungry, and the two men gave them food and warm blankets, but they would not allow them to touch even one of the lustrous gems that sparkled around them.

At last the Chinamen went away quite rested, and with plenty of food in their sacks. They had gone only a short distance, down the cañon, when in the darkest shadow the giant stopped.

"Let us rest here," he said, "and talk over our plans for the future. There is a great treasure near us, I am strong, you are active, and we are separated from our wishes by only two men of ordinary strength."

The dwarf sighed heavily. "They have been kind to us, but for them we must have died of hunger."

"Fool," replied the giant, "there is enough for all."

Then it was they sat talking till the stronger prevailed over the weaker, and, at the still hour of midnight, they went back to the cavern of gold.

The dwarf had begged hard for the lives

of the men, but the cruel giant was obdurate.

"Let them die," he said, "and the treasure will be ours."

In the darkness he struck the blow, but instead of falling upon the men, as he had intended, he struck the stone on which their heads had rested. A harsh ringing sound resounded through the cavern, and suddenly a great light flashed up, and almost blinded them, so that they covered their eyes with their hands.

When a moment after they glanced fearfully around, they saw not two common men, but two horrid monsters. Whether immense giants or genii, they could not tell, but the giant Chinaman before them seemed but a boy in size.

The poor Chinamen trembled with fear, and begged the monsters to spare their lives.

"I did not wish to kill you," said the dwarf. "Oh, dear! have pity! have pity! and he clasped his little hands imploringly; while his teeth chattered with the intensity of his fear.

"You would have robbed us," replied the monster, "and for this you shall be punished."

Then he laid a spell upon them, condemning them to remain far from their beloved China. Wandering through the gold land, and finding treasures, but never possessing them.

To the dwarf he said, " because the good had not all gone out of your heart, you may be permitted to aid the future gold-seekers, and they shall be blessed by your guidance. But a curse shall follow the gifts of the giant, and his bones shall bleach upon the mountains of the stranger land."

"Strive by deeds of kindness, poor dwarf," he continued, "to wipe out the stain of this present great sin of your life, so that at last, when you die, your body may be wafted to the pleasant shore of the celestial country."

Then he drove them out of the cave, and they began their weary wanderings. The giant filled with angry bitterness, and the heart of the dwarf subdued and penitent.

For some time after the merchant had finished his story, Ching Chong sat in silence. At last he exclaimed, eagerly, "who knows but they are now in the gold-land to which I am going."

"I had thought of that," answered the old man. "It may be all a myth, but as you say 'who knows!' At all events there is no harm in my saying, *beware of the giant, and look out for the dwarf.*"

Just as the ship was about sailing, the merchant gave to Ching Chong a curious black wand, saying, "this is a divining-rod, and will help you to find the treasure. Remember all I have said to you. Espe-cially *beware of the giant.*"

Again Ching Chong promised, and they embraced with much affection.

At last the signal was given, the anchor weighed, and the merchant hastened on shore, to look out upon the waters, till Ching Chong, leaning over the railing of the deck, faded from his sight.

Thus Ching Chong became a gold-seeker, and many were the gorgeous dreams that filled the mind of the youth, as the ship sailed lazily over the placid waters.

At last, after the usual amount of winds and calms, storms and fair weather, the good ship sailed through the Golden Gate, and into the pleasant harbor of San Francisco.

Ching Chong disembarked with the other passengers, a stranger in a land of strangers, where even the language of the country fell upon his ear, the unmeaning jargon of an unknown tongue.

Fortunately for him, he was not the only Chinaman in the country, though at that early day they were few in number. The Queen city of the Pacific was then a city of many sand hills, and a few poor shanties, but it was full of energy, perseverance, and hope.

Ching Chong was a quick, active lad, and soon learned enough of English to procure a situation, and for some time remained in San Francisco.

At night, when his work was over, he would take a look at his divining-rod, and he often noticed it would turn in his hand, till it pointed to the mountain country, awaking all the wild dreams, and eager longings that in the leisure hours of the sea-voyage filled his imagination.

At last he could resist the impulse no longer, and joined a party of prospectors for the mining districts.

For months Ching Chong wandered over the mountains with his comrades, till his shoes were worn out, and his trousers and blue shirt so patched with flour-sacks, that it was impossible for the uninitiated to distinguish the original material.

Still he found nothing, even the divining-rod seemed to have lost its power, save when he was alone.

One night he sat apart from the others, feeling very sad, and wishing he had never left China. The homesick longing to see his native land growing continually in his heart, oppressed him greatly.

The thought of the kind old merchant who had been as a father to him, pursued him, but deeper down in his heart was cherished the memory of the merchant's daughter. The gentle Ah Zore maiden with the almond-shaped eyes, and tiny feet.

Just as he was yielding himself to tender dreams, his wand rested upon his bosom, and there he felt his secret talisman, the divining-rod.

Rising up hastily, he resolved to go off alone, and yield to the impulse of the wand. Hoping he might be more successful than in the weary months he had passed with his companions.

With this resolve, the pressure of the rod became greater, awaking joyous hopes that had long been strangers to him.

He thought of the curious legend the merchant had told him, and whispering

softly to himself, he said: "Where the
wand leads I will go—on to fortune, or
death; any thing is better than the weariness of my present life."

It was a beautiful, balmy night. The
silvery moonlight and the stars brightened even the dim cavern, and flooded
the mountains with a luminous beauty.

Ching Chong went silently up the mountain path until he came to a ledge the
miners had been prospecting that day.

Still the divining-rod urged him on, till
he had gone miles farther into the mountains than ever before.

About twelve o'clock, he began to be
hungry and weary, for it was the early
evening when he started, and after a hard
day's work.

Suddenly the divining-rod changed, and
pointed downward, and as Ching Chong
looked, he saw what appeared to be the

entrance of a cavern, but a huge stone was rolled against it.

He perceived a small opening which the stone left uncovered, through which he might have crept, but the darkness within was so dense that he dare not enter.

He threw himself down upon the ground quite overcome with hunger and fatigue, and taking a piece of hard bread from his pocket, began eating, and thinking almost hopelessly of the future.

He was aroused by a harsh voice, and looking up, saw, just before him, the immense form of a giant Chinaman.

"What are you doing here, countryman," said the giant, opening his huge mouth, and glaring with his ugly eyes upon the startled boy.

"I am thinking of home," replied Ching Chong, sadly, "and fearing I shall never see that dearest spot again."

"Thank God, the bodies of all true Chinamen are carried back to repose in death in the bosom of their mother-land."

" Do you mean to insult me, minion," cried the giant, while his face grew livid with rage, and he would have killed Ching Chong with one blow of his heavy club, but the boy sprang lightly out of his way.

" Foiled again," he muttered, between his teeth. " Come here, boy," he added, " I will not hurt you, silly fool."

"I was only joking, just to see you jump out of the way ;" and he gave a loud laugh that made the mountains echo.

The rod in his bosom urging him on, Ching Chong drew cautiously near the giant.

" Sit down, and tell me of your wanderings," said the monster, with a rough voice, into which he tried to throw the semblance of kindness.

Ching Chong told him all, only omitting the merchant's story and his secret of the wand.

"Never mind, boy," said the giant, " you shall win the prize, and go back to China a rich man. See, the morning sun is rising. Now we will enter the cavern, and you shall have as much gold and precious stones as you can carry away.

Ching Chong felt a momentary thrill of joy in his heart, which was saddened by the memory of the merchant's last words, " beware of the giant."

"I have wandered in this cold, stranger land for three long years, and found nothing until now.

" Wealth is within my grasp; if I do not seize it, I may never have another chance! To be poor forever! No! no! I will take the risk." Then he spoke aloud, in a resolute voice, "Lead on, I will follow."

The giant gave the great stone a push with his foot, and rolled it away as though it had been a pebble.

As they entered he struck a torch, then, before proceeding, rolled back the stone and closed up the opening.

When Ching Chong saw himself shut into the cave with the giant, he trembled with fear, for he saw there was no way of escape. He felt now, he had only to follow where the monster at will might lead him.

They went through a long, narrow passage, then down many steps, until at last they entered a hall, which was lighted by a large lamp, suspended from the dome of the cavern.

Ching Chong was almost blinded by the reflection of the luminous crystals that, with curious prismatic effect, flooded the hall with a hundred glowing tints.

Great masses of gold lay scattered about,

and huge seams ran through the rugged sides of the cavern.

"Is this rich enough for you?" said the giant, laughingly.

"Help yourself, lad, you remember I told you you should have all you could carry away."

The delighted Ching Chong began to gather up the gold and precious stones into his sack, and when he had secured all he could carry, throwing the sack over his shoulder, he thanked the giant, and begged him to let him go out of the cave.

"Go on!" replied the giant, with a mocking laugh. "You're welcome to the treasure, but I'm thinking you'll find it hard work to move that stone from the mouth of the cave."

Then Ching Chong threw down the treasure at his feet, crying, with tears in his eyes, "Take back your riches, and let me

go out into the sunshine! the beautiful
sunshine! Oh! good giant, take back
your gold, and give me my poverty, and
my liberty!"

"What a pretty actor! go on! go on!"
said the delighted giant, and when Ching
Chong threw himself on his knees before
him, wringing his hands in silent despair,
he laughed till the mountain cavern rung.

"Do you think I will let you go? You
are my slave now! and the sunshine! the
beautiful sunshine! you shall never see
again."

Ching Chong saw there was no help for
him then.

He spurned the bag of gold and precious
stones, pushing it with his foot, as he followed the giant into the inner cave.

The giant ordered him to build a fire,
and prepare supper, and, after the master
was served, he was permitted to eat and

go to sleep upon the rough but warm skin of a grizzly bear.

Weeks passed by! Still he was a prisoner in the cavern, serving the grim old giant, who was very capricious, and hard to please.

One evening he came home in great good humor, and, while he ate his supper, he talked and laughed with Ching Chong very pleasantly.

He told how that day he had given a quantity of gold to some miners.

"Great luck it will bring them," he added.

"Already they are quarreling over it," and a malicious grin disfigured his monstrous face.

"'Tis such fools as you, boy, who make things lively. Ha! ha! You may have all the gold you can carry away!

"Why don't you move the stone? Ah!

boy, if you had the famous divining-rod, you would only have to touch the rock, and it would obey your wish, but you might as well hope to wake up in your beloved China, as to obtain it."

How strangely the words of the giant thrilled the heart of Ching Chong, and, pressing his hand against his bosom, the famous divining-rod awakened the hopes that in his heart lay sleeping.

In the excess of his emotion he was obliged to hide his face from the giant, lest he should see his secret written there.

That night after the loud snoring of the giant announced that he was sleeping soundly, Ching Chong rose carefully, and lighting the torch, crept softly out of the large cave, and through the narrow passage that led to the entrance.

He took nothing with him. " The treasure of the giant is cursed," he said.

5

When he came to the rock he took the
divining-rod from his bosom, and, pressing
it lightly against the rock, said : " Giant
rock remove quickly at the spell of the
divining-rod."

Quick as thought the rock moved from
its place, and the silver moonlight poured
in at the entrance of the cave, and lighted
up the face of Ching Chong, beaming with
the bliss of recovered liberty.

Once more he touched the rock, saying :
" Move back giant rock at the spell of the
the divining-rod, and remain forever so
firmly fixed that even the giant's powerful
hand cannot remove you."

The great stone rolled back, striking the
ledge with such force that the whole mountain shook, and the mighty echo was rever-
berated from all the neighboring heights.

This great commotion aroused the sleeping giant, and he called loudly for Ching

Chong, and, when he received no answer, he was very much enraged, and searched the whole cavern in every nook and corner. At last he rushed to the entrance, and pushed his broad shoulder against the rock, but he could not move it one inch from its place; then he became so furious that his voice sounded like the roar of a wild beast, but with all his efforts he could not move the rock. Ching Chong sat without in the calm moonlight, now and then calling to the giant to come on, and that he was welcome to all the treasure he could bring with him.

After a time the giant became so exhausted that he ceased his efforts to move the rock, and begged Ching Chong to touch it again with his magic wand, and let him out, promising him all the treasures of the cave; but the boy only replied: "Your turn has come now, keep your treas-

G 2 I 0 1 1 5

ure, you are welcome to it, and to your underground castle."

"Good-by, kind master, good-by! Come out when you can, and you may have all the treasure you can carry."

With this Ching Chong started for his old cabin, but for miles the deep howlings of the giant were wafted to his ears.

He reached the cabin at sunrise, just five weeks after he left it.

When he entered he found his old companions just eating breakfast. They were greatly surprised to see him, for they supposed he had been killed by the grizzly bears with which that district abounded.

They gave him a hearty greeting, and he sat down to breakfast, telling them only the last of his marvelous adventures, omitting the secret of the divining-rod entirely.

When he had finished, he asked them what luck they had had.

Nothing very good, they replied. Some placer diggings of a little promise, but their fortunes were not yet made.

Ching Chong went out with them, and entered again upon the hard life of prospecting. Many months passed on in the same old way, and again Ching Chong began to feel very much disheartened. Four years and a half had gone, and still he was poor, no nearer the realization of his dreams than ever.

The intense longing for home was ever gnawing in his heart. He thought sadly of the old merchant who awaited his return, and sighed often as he dreamed of the beautiful Ah Zore.

Again he resolved to follow the guiding of the divining-rod, hoping for greater success than in his former expedition.

Again he started at nightfall, without saying any thing to his companions.

He had provided himself with a sack of food, which he carried, with his pick and shovel, upon his shoulders.

He was young, healthy, and accustomed to the hardships of a mountain life.

For hours he walked on as the divining-rod guided him, until near morning, when, overcome with fatigue, he threw himself upon the ground among the thick sage brush, and soon fell asleep.

A thousand golden imaginings mingled with his dreams, and, when he awoke with the sunshine pouring its flood of warmth and light upon him, he rose full of bright hopes, ate his scanty breakfast, and started upon his way with a happy heart.

Thus he wandered on for several days, carefully examining every ledge of rocks that he passed over.

His stock of food was nearly exhausted. The divining-rod and his hopeful nature urged him on, but his dread of a lonely death in the mountains warned him to return.

One night he struck a fire in a lonely place, and sat down to eat his supper, just as the twilight gave place to the stars of night.

He was getting quite disheartened. "I must start for the camp in the morning," he said to himself, " 'Tis no use of trying any longer."

He fell into a sad train of musing, from which he was aroused by the soft tinkling of a silver bell, and looking up he saw before him the dwarf Chinaman.

He wore the round hat, blue blouse, big pants, and pointed shoes of the Celestials, and his words fell upon Ching Chong's ear in the language of his native tongue. His face was wrinkled and sad-looking, yet there was a kindliness in its expression, and Ching Chong's heart warmed as he pleasantly asked, "Why so sorrowful to-night, my boy?"

Then Ching Chong told his story.

When he had finished the dwarf said: "Be thankful that you did not attempt to carry away any of the treasure."

"If you had taken but one ounce of gold the wand would have lost its power in your hand, and you would have been the slave of the giant as long as you lived, and after death your bones would have whitened the floor of the mountain cavern, instead of reposing in the dear native land."

"Your industry and perseverance shall now be rewarded. Lie down and sleep to-night upon this soft turf. In the morning rise and follow the direction of the divining-rod, and where it points downward strike your pick."

"Now good-night, my boy. In the days of your prosperity, sometimes think kindly of the poor dwarf of the mountains."

Before Ching Chong could reply, he found himself alone, and though he looked round carefully, he could not discover where, or how the dwarf had disappeared. So he lay down, and was soon sleeping soundly.

In the morning he rose early, and following the direction of his wand, stopped where it pointed downward, and striking a blow with his pick, turned up a beautiful pure nugget of gold.

He marked the spot, and collecting a few specimens, returned to the camp.

Again his companions surrounded him to hear his story.

No one but the poor, toiling miner can understand the excitement and delight of the weary prospectors, as they listened to him, and examined his specimens.

5*

"Now, boys," said Ching Chong, "you have been the sharers of my bad luck, and you shall share my good fortune."

"There is gold enough for all."

Then the happy miners all shook hands with Ching Chong, saying a hearty "God bless you, boy," while the tears glistened in their eyes, as they thought of the dear ones in distant lands.

That night they all dreamed golden dreams, full of love and happiness.

In the morning they all went together to the newly discovered treasure, which proved to be a large tract of the richest placer-diggings ever known.

In six months they were all rich men, and left the mountains for their different homes, blessing forever Ching Chong Chinaman.

About that time a good ship sailed for China, and on the deck sat the happy

Ching Chong, and all his great wealth was on board.

After a prosperous voyage, he reached his dear, native land, and was able to give his friend the merchant, an account of himself, so satisfactory that he rewarded him with the hand of his daughter, the beautiful Ah Zore, and in all Hong Kong there could not be found a happier man than Ching Chong Chinaman.

ZALETTA.

ONCE upon a time there lived in a little cane hut on the borders of a hacienda, a poor old Mexican woman and her grandchild.

The parents of the little one were both dead, and the old woman maintained herself and the child by spinning, sewing, and washing for the rich Spaniards, to whom all the fine houses and cultivated lands of the country belonged.

The mother of the child had been a beautiful senorita of good family. She foolishly loved and married the poor but light-hearted Mexican, who would have given his life for her, but could not shield her from the misfortunes which poverty and sickness brought upon them.

After the birth of her little daughter, she died, and very soon the father was lost in a fearful storm at sea; so the child was left alone in the world, with none to care for her but the silver-haired grandmother, and no home but the little cane hut.

For some years every thing went pleasantly with the child; she had never known luxury, her necessities were supplied, she returned the fond devotion of the old grandmother, with the ardor of her Southern nature; and, all day long, her innocent voice, full of childish happiness, woke cheerful echoes around the little hut.

One night, when she was about ten years old, the old woman fell sick. She felt the dim shadows creeping over her spirit, and her strength growing less;-and calling the child to her side, she said, feebly: "I have

nothing but a well-worn distaff and the
poor hut to give you. The Holy Virgin
pity and protect you; you have been a
good child to your old grandmother." Then
she kissed her, and blessing her, bade her
good-night, adding: "Never forget to say
your prayers before you go to sleep. God
bless you, my poor, poor child."

The grandmother turned her face to the
wall, and folded her thin hands as if in
prayer, and Zaletta crept softly into bed
beside her, feeling very sad; but soon her
innocent heart was happy, roaming through
the pleasant land of dreams. In the morning, Zaletta slept till the sun rose above
the hills, and cast its glowing warmth down
into the shaded valleys, then woke full of
life and joyousness.

There lay the grandmother just as she
had last seen her the night before. "She
sleeps long this morning, the dear old

grandmother," said she to herself, as she moved round quietly, preparing the scanty breakfast.

When it was all ready, she became impatient, and laid her little warm hand upon the old woman's arm. Cold, very cold, the poor child found her, and motionless. She would never move again.

Zaletta called her, sobbing and weeping, but there was no reply. The heart so ready to sympathize with all her childish sorrows was at rest. The old grandmother had died, praying for the little lonely child, who had been dearer than all the world to her.

The next day the people from the hacienda, came and buried the old woman. After the last sod was cast upon the grave, the innkeeper's wife took the child by the hand, saying: "Poor little thing, she can not stay here alone, I will take her home with me;" and she smoothed the tangled hair of the helpless orphan with her hand, and in her harder heart she thought, "By and by this girl may be made of great service to me, and even now I'll see that she earns all that she eats and wears."

She was very careful to take to the inn with her, all the poor little hut contained. "'Tis but little," she said, "but I'll take it for the child." All the neighbors said it was kind in the innkeeper's wife, and the rich senor, to whom the whole hacienda belonged, gave her a shining gold-piece, saying: "'Tis for your charity."

The cold-hearted woman went home, leading by the hand a little weeping child, very desolate and sorrowful.

The innkeeper was naturally a kind man, but he had become too indolent and corpulent to resist the strong will of his termagant wife. When he saw the sad-

eyed little one that she had brought home,
he brushed away a tear with his big brown
hand, and determined to save the unfortu-
nate from all trouble, as much as he could;
but when he thought of his wife's cruel
disposition, he earnestly wished her in
other hands.

"Poor little thing! poor little thing!"
he said, pityingly, and calling his own little
boy and girl to him, he placed her trembling hands in theirs, adding: "Here is a
sister for you, be kind to her, my children."

The daughter drew her hand away, and
curled her lip in scorn. She was like her
mother, proud and cold in her nature, and,
looking at the coarse clothes of the child,
she said: "Ah, no, papa, she is only fit
for a servant. Sister, indeed!" and she
shook the skirts of her pretty muslin dress,
and ran away.

The boy felt the manhood dawning in his heart, as he saw the tears glistening in the pretty dark eyes of the silent child, and the little red lips quivered with suppressed emotion.

" She shall be my sister, papa," said he, softly, as he took her by the hand, and led her out in the clear sunshine. Children understand each other best, thought the old man, as he sat watching them, while they walked up and down the garden together, talking pleasantly.

Soon the mother's sharp eye detected them, and with a harsh voice she bade the little girl haste to the kitchen, and see if she could not help the cook prepare the supper.

Then she called the young Guilerme to her, saying: " I hope to make a rich senor of you, my son, though your father is only an innkeeper. We are making money, and every year increases our gains. There is good blood in my veins, and I am determined to raise my children above my present condition. For this I save every thing. Every thing! For we must have money; but remember, my son, I would not have you notice that miserable girl I have brought here for a servant; by and by she may do for your sister's maid; now she is the kitchen scullion."

Thus began the days of servitude and sorrow for the young Zaletta.

The inn was a spacious adobe house, with an open court in the center, and surrounded on all sides by a broad piazza. The kitchen and store-rooms were upon one side, while the receiving and sleeping rooms were on the other sides of the square.

The hacienda was in the southern part of California, where though the warmth of the days produces many kinds of tropical fruits, the evenings are often quite chilly, and the excessive heat of the noon-day renders all very susceptible to cold. In the large receiving-room (with the bar at one side), on such nights, a cheerful fire always burned, and there all the guests of the house assembled, and talked over the news of the day. Sometimes 'twas of the discovery of a rich gold mine, but often 'twas of a fearful robbery in the wood.

After all the work was done in the kitchen, Zaletta would steal silently into the receiving-room, listening to the conversation, and warming her chilled feet and hands before going to her miserable bed in the out-house.

This did not please the senora. It did not look respectable to have the miserable child about, she would say; but in this the innkeeper was resolute. "The little one

should warm herself before going to bed."
So Zaletta came in at evenings, but very
quietly.

Guilerme was always kind to her; indeed
never a day passed but something nice
found its way to the hiding-place in the
outhouse, so that the child was never
hungry.

He brought her the ripest bananas, and
the sweetest oranges, and when she would
look up to him, with her soft eyes dewy
with love and thanks, he would kiss her
brown cheek, and say: "Never mind, little one, you shall be *senora* one of these
days." Then they would laugh and be
happy, till the mother's sharp voice would
ring through the house, calling the unfortu-
nate to some new task.

The sister was changeful in her treatment
to Zaletta. Sometimes she would call her
pleasantly to come and play with her, but

very soon she would become angry and strike her, calling her "only a pitiful servant." Then the mother would whip Zaletta for making her little mistress angry. The father and Guilerme always took her part, making the mother more displeased than ever.

One day, when Guilerme was about fourteen years old, and the girls were twelve, the mother called the boy to her, telling him in two weeks a vessel would sail from the nearest sea-port for the Atlantic States, and that he must be ready to take passage in her, for she had determined to send him to New York to school. "Your father is now rich," she said, "and you must be educated like other rich men's sons."

Poor little Zaletta! What a blow it was to her. Her best friend going away so far over the waters. When he told her the morning before he sailed what his mother had said, her pretty dark eyes filled with tears, and she sobbed bitterly.

"Listen to me," said the boy, soothingly; "I have something to tell you, and must be quick, or mamma will call me before I can finish. You know I am going away to be educated like a gentleman, and shall want a lady for my wife; so you must study hard to become one, for I am determined to marry you as soon as I come back. I have taught you to read, and you will find all my books in the hiding-place, where I have left them for you, and you must study hard and see how beautiful you can grow while I am gone, for I shall make you the greatest lady in the hacienda;" and he took the little eager face between his hands and kissed it with much affection. Just then the mother called, "Guilerme! Guilerme!" so he kissed her again, and said, "remember, my little wife," and was off in a moment.

That night Zaletta wept herself to sleep, and many succeeding nights; but she did not forget to study very hard, and though she labored under great difficulties, her progress was wonderful. She was working for the approval of the only one that loved her since the dear silver-haired grandmother died. After Guilerme went away the senora took Zaletta into the house as maid for her young daughter, who every day was growing more proud and selfish.

For some years the innkeeper had been greatly prospered. The family had used economy in all things until they had amassed considerable wealth.

"Now," said the senora, "the children are growing up, and we must not spare the money—they must have position." She engaged a governess to teach her daughter, and a master to give her lessons on the harp and guitar.

Zaletta always sat in the room with the young senorita, and listened eagerly to every word the teachers uttered, though her hands were busy with her needle.

Every day she grew in knowledge and beauty. Her dark eyes were soft as a fawn's, and her pure olive cheek glowed with a clear rose-tint, while her form and features were cast in beauty's most exquisite mold. Both mother and daughter were often cruelly unkind to her, more especially when they saw that her beauty, and innocent sweetness of manner, attracted more attention than all the young senorita's fine clothes and accomplishments. The senorita was pretty and full of airs and graces, but Zaletta, in her coarse dress, was far more lovely. Every day increased the

6

envy of the mother and daughter, and new and harder tasks were invented for the weary little hands to perform.

One sultry afternoon all three sat upon the piazza of the inner court. A ship had arrived from New York, with letters from Guilerme, and a large box, filled with beautiful fabrics for dresses, shawls, and ornaments, for the mother and daughter; but Zaletta received nothing, not even a word of kind remembrance.

All the long night before she had wept. Guilerme, the gentleman, had forgotten the poor maid; but she, alas! remembered him too well.

The mother and daughter sat looking over their treasures with great delight, and for the time she was unnoticed. Stitching away upon a beautiful organdie muslin, at last overcome by fatigue, loss of sleep, and the excessive heat, she fell asleep, and in her dreams she called out in a piteous tone, "Guilerme! Guilerme!" and the tears ran down her pale cheeks.

"What is she saying?" said the mother. She rose and looked at her, and again she called, "Guilerme! Guilerme!"

"Hear her, mamma," exclaimed the enraged daughter, "I'll give her a lesson for her impertinence," and she raised her hand to strike the sleeping girl.

"Stop, daughter," said the mother, softly, with a malicious smile, "we can do better. The foolish Guilerme has sent her a letter and presents of books. The letter I have burned. The books you can do as you like with, but I have a present for la senorita, she will not like, perhaps."

She shook the young girl roughly by the arm, saying, "What, sleeping over your work. Wake, and hear what Guilerme says. He sends you this!"

The senora held out to the young girl a coarse apron, such as the lower servants wore. " He hopes his sister will train you to be a good servant for you must know he is in love with a rich and beautiful senorita, and though they are both young now, it is thought best for them to be married before his return, which will be in about two years."

" Mamma, what is the matter with her ? How pale she looks !" cried the affrighted daughter, as Zaletta with closed eyes sank fainting upon the floor.

She has fainted, the miserable beggar. To try to creep into my family, and to think that foolish boy should talk of love to her. I'll fix them both," and in her anger the senora and her daughter left Zaletta lying cold and pale upon the floor.

Evening came on, with the calm, silver light of the stars, before Zaletta recovered.

At first she could not remember what had happened, and then it all rushed upon her, a mighty flood of sorrow.

" Guilerme has forgotten me! I remember now : this apron for the servant of his bride. Ah! Guilerme! Guilerme!" Wrapping the apron about her neck, she rushed out into the night. " I cannot stay in this house another night. It will kill me! she said, and she hurried on as though she could fly from her great sorrow.

At last she came to a deep wood, and, after wandering about till her wearied limbs refused to carry her any further, she saw a light glimmering through the trees, and pressing on she came to a little cottage.

Looking in at the window she saw an old woman at her distaff spinning. The faggots upon the hearth burned brightly, and lighted up the little room, but especially the face of the old woman shone with the glow of a kind heart. Timidly she knocked at the door, but there was no reply. Then she knocked again louder, and the old woman called out in a cracked voice: "Who knocks at my door so late in the night!"

"Only a poor maiden, who has no home, no friend on earth. I pray you, good woman, let me in. The night is cold, and the starlight chills me. I am so tired! so tired! Good mother, let me in!"

The old woman opened the door and led her in. She sat down in the corner, gazing silently into the fire and wondering why the good Lord in pity did not let her die; and big tears ran down her pale cheeks.

The old woman baked a fresh tortilla and gave it to her with a cup of milk.

"Eat, child," she said gently, "you are hungry," and she laid her hand on the bowed head, saying again: "There! there! eat, child! and sleep away the sorrow of youth which is fleeting as the dew of morning."

Then she turned away and commenced spinning and singing in a low, monotonous tone, which was strangely soothing, while Zaletta ate her supper, and soon the sad, weary maiden fell asleep by the warm, pleasant fireside.

For some time the old woman went on spinning and singing, till another knock came at the door, and again she said: "Who knocks at my door so late in the night? " 'Tis I, mother," replied a thick, rough voice. She opened the door to a most curious looking dwarf. He was round shouldered and thick set, with heavy, black hair covering his forehead, and shaggy brows meeting over his eyes.

"How fared thee, to-day, son?"

"I haven't struck the lode yet, mother," said the dwarf, cheerfully, "but I am sure the mine is rich. See what I have picked up among the loose rocks!'

He handed her a small nugget of gold, almost pure, and turned to the corner to put down his pick and shovel. "But who have we here? A young girl, and very pretty," he added, looking admiringly upon the sleeping maiden.

"Only a poor friendless child, who came to the door a little while ago, weeping and asking shelter," answered the woman.

"Treat her kindly, mother; she will be company for you, and by-and-by I may marry her, but I have no time to think of women now."

The dwarf sat down to the hot supper the mother had prepared for him, and ate heartily, for he was very hungry. Then he drew his chair near the fire, and sat for sometime looking dreamily into its glowing embers.

"I must strike the lode soon," he mused. "Oh, my rich gold mine; it must come at last." Then he rose, saying, kindly, "Good night, mother," and climbed up into the little loft, where in a few minutes he was sleeping soundly.

The old woman woke Zaletta, and they retired for the night, sleeping in the same bed.

In the morning Zaletta was awakened by a kind voice calling, "Get up now, daughter, and help me to prepare my son's breakfast, he has been at work for an hour, and will soon come in very hungry."

Zaletta rose quickly and helped to prepare a breakfast of fresh tortillas nicely browned, fried plantain, and venison, which, with plenty of ripe fruit and goat's milk, made a repast fit for a prince.

6*

Soon the dwarf came in, so smiling and cheerful, that though Zaletta thought him the ugliest looking person she ever saw, she felt sure his heart was in the right place. You are welcome, my pretty girl," he said, "but don't mind me; I've no time to compliment women, though by-and-by, when I strike a rich lode, I may marry you."

Zaletta's face flushed a deep crimson, and she looked as though that would be any thing but desirable; but she made no reply, and in a moment the dwarf seemed to have forgotten her presence, and she became more comfortable.

Two years passed by and Zaletta remained at the cottage, helping the old mother, who was very fond of her, and reading books with which the dwarf kept her constantly supplied. All this time he was working hard in his mine, but could not " strike the rich lode." Sometimes he

grew quite disheartened, then he would be
joyous and hopeful, and would say to
Zaletta : "Though I have no time to think
of women now, by-and-by, when I am rich,
I will marry you." She soon got used to
this, and only laughed, for he was always
very kind to her, and she learned to look
upon him as a brother.

One dark night in the rainy season she
and the mother sat by the fire waiting for
the dwarf to come in to his supper. The
old woman was spinning, and Zaletta reading a pleasant book of travels.

"My poor boy," sighed the old mother.
"How it rains; he will be wet through.
Oh, dear! I fear he will never be able to
strike the rich lode." Just then a loud
knock came at the door. "Who knocks
at my door so late in the night," said the
old woman.

A voice, young, strong, and pure, an-

swered, sending all the warm blood from
Zaletta's heart to her face: " A stranger,
belated and lost in the wood, begs for
shelter from the storm."

The old woman opened the door, and
Guilerme—dear, handsome Guilerme, dripping with rain, and very cold, entered.

Zaletta's book dropped upon the floor,
and her tongue refused her heart utterance, but Guilerme's eyes rested upon the
beautiful girl with delighted surprise.

"Found at last, my own Zaletta." His
arms opened, and the trembling, lonely
heart of the maiden found its true resting-
place.

They sat down side by side, hand clasping hand, and explained all the past to
each other, how Guilerme had written and
received no answer, and at last returned to
find her gone, and his heart desolate.

Zaletta told him all she had suffered, and

of the kindness she had received at the cottage. Then Guilerme took the old woman's hands and thanked her with a voice trembling with emotion.

The mother rejoiced with them, but there mingled a sorrow for her son with the joy. "Poor son," she thought, "He is very fond of the child."

Soon another knock came, and again the old woman asked, "Who knocks at my door so late in the night," and the dwarf answered:—

"Mother! mother! I've struck the lode at last."

She opened the door, and he threw his arms round her neck and kissed her, then he came in, and saw Guilerme; and they both told their stories.

"So," said the dwarf, when Guilerme had finished: "You have come to take my pretty maid away? Well, if she loves you, 'tis all right, I have had no time to think of women; but, somehow, I have grown fond of her," and he sighed heavily. "I have struck the lode at last. I am a rich man, but I must find some one to share my good fortune with me, some pure, good little girl like our Zaletta."

In the morning, when Guilerme and the dwarf went to the mine together, they found it even richer than the dwarf had thought it, the night before. Guilerme offered to furnish the money to build a mill to crush the ore, for one-half the mine; and so they became partners.

Soon after this, Guilerme and Zaletta were married at the cottage in the wood, and in time the good dwarf was united to a pretty Mexican lass, who made him very happy.

After a time, Guilerme built a fine house for his wife, and, when they had two little children, he took his family home to the old hacienda.

The mother and sister did not recognize their old servant in Guilerme's brilliant senora, but the old father (God bless him) knew her, when she placed her little soft hand in his, and kissed him; and very dearly he learned to love his dutiful daughter.

So they were all rich and happy, as long as it pleased God to spare their lives.

THE STRONG MAN OF SANTA BARBARA.

MANY years ago, in the old Spanish mission of Santa Barbara, lived an old Mexican, named Joza Silva, with his wife and child, in a little adobe house, containing but one room.

There was a small window, rudely latticed with unplaned laths, and a door opening upon a pleasant view of the golden-sanded beach and the restless waves of the ocean.

At that time, the Spaniards, Mexicans, and Indians were the only inhabitants of the country.

Over these people, the padres, who established the mission, had acquired a most unlimited sway, ruling them more completely than even the Pope his subjects of the Holy See of Rome.

The Mexicans are an indolent race. The luxurious climate of Santa Barbara is not favorable to the development of latent energy in any people, least of all to the inert Mexicans; yet the padres, by awakening their superstitious fears, made them work until the wilderness became a vineyard, and the golden orange glowed amid the leaves of the fragrant trees.

Poor Joza disliked any exertion, and, if left to his own inclination, would have lived on the spontaneous productions of that almost tropical climate, and been happy after his oyster fashion.

Often he obeyed very reluctantly, those whom he thought had power, not only over the body, but could doom his soul to unnumbered years of suffering, in the fearful fires of purgatory

The padres lived in great ease and comfort; though so far from the elegances of the great world, their own ingenuity and the rapid growth of the country, furnished them with many luxuries.

Their quaint adobe houses were very pleasant, built after the Spanish style, in the form of a square with an open court in the center.

Beautiful gardens flourished around them, in which grew the fragrant citron, the lemon, with its shining leaves, and nearly all the rare fruits and flowers of the tropics.

For some years, Joza labored in the vineyards and gardens; but the ambitious padres were planning a greater work. A new church was ta be built, and elaborate-ly ornamented; a convent and college was planned; extensive grounds to be laid out and cultivated, and all to be surrounded by the enduring adobe wall of mud and stones.

One evening, after a weary day in the vineyard, just as Joza was about starting for home, padre Antonio called him.

" On the morrow," he said, " we will begin to lay the foundation of the new church, the Grand San Pedro; you shall be permitted to aid in the blessed work, by carrying stones and mortar, for which great mercy thank the holy Mother and all the saints, especially the blessed San Pedro, who is the patron saint of this great enterprise."

Then the padre blessed him, and wandered off into the delicious shade of the garden.

In the gathering gloom of the twilight, Joza returned to his cottage, more disheartened than ever, wondering how much more torturing the fires of purgatory could be, than carrying stones under the burning sun of Santa Barbara.

As he approached his cottage, he saw his wife sitting before the door with a stranger, both smoking, with the greatest apparent enjoyment.

His son, and a large dog, were rolling about on the soft earth, near them, raising a cloud of dust, and making a great noise, which seemed to disturb no one, and to afford them much pleasure.

When Joza came up, his wife introduced the stranger as his old playmate, and her brother Schio, who, many years before, had gone away, and, until that evening, had never been heard from.

Joza welcomed his old friend in the cordial Spanish way, placing his house at his disposal.

For a short time, in pleasant memories of

their boyhood, he forgot the weary present. After they had eaten their frugal supper, and were again seated in the vine-clad doorway, Joza looked out upon the great ocean, dusky with the shadows of evening, growing sad and silent.

" What ails thee, brother," said Schio, in his clear, ringing voice, that sounded like the strong notes of a clarionet. " You are changed; you are growing old, but see me, I am as young in heart as your boy, and strong as a bullock."

He lifted a great stone that lay near him, and held it at arms' length, laughing loudly, till the caves of the ocean sent back a hundred echoes.

With many sighs, Joza told the story of his troubles; how, for years, till his back had grown old and stiff, he had worked in the vineyard of the padre, but the purple harvest had brought no blessing to him.

How a harder task was to be laid upon him. He was to hew and carry the heavy foundation-stones of the Grand San Pedro, and even at the thought of so great labor, the beaded sweat rolled down his forehead.

His sympathizing wife sobbed aloud, but the brother only laughed, till again he woke the mysterious voices of the ocean caves.

Half angry, Joza turned to Schio, saying: " 'Tis all very well for you, Schio, to laugh; you who roam at will in the cool of the evening, and rest in the delightful shade, while the scorching sunshine is burning my life out."

Poor Joza buried his face in his hands and sighed wearily.

"Cheer up, brother," said Schio, pleas-antly. "Listen to me. Go in the morning, to padre Antonio, and tell him you are getting old and feeble, and cannot work through the heat of the day, but if he will appoint your task, you will accomplish it after the burning sun has gone down.

"Tell him if you carry those large stones in the day, your life will be consumed like the burning candles before the altar; but that in the cool of the evening, your strength returns as in the days of youth."

"And what, then?" said Joza, wearily.

"I will see that the morning finds your task accomplished," replied Schio.

That night Joza dreamed that his tasks were ended, and that all day long he luxuriated in most delicious ease, under the shade of olive trees, and, when he woke, his heart grew sad, that it was only a dream.

He rose in haste to go to his task, for he had overslept himself; then he thought of Schio's advice. "I will do as he told me, though I fear 'twill do no good," thought he. "I can but fail, and who knows what may come.

"Schio is such a strange fellow; when he's talking, it seems as though a hundred voices rung changes on his words. God grant he's not in league with the devil."

Joza crossed himself, and muttered prayers most devoutly until he reached the house of the padre Antonio.

After he had told the padre all Schio had directed, his task was appointed, and he returned home, all day long resting in the shade of his favorite lime-tree, smoking his cigarettés, and was happy as only a careless, indolent Mexican could be, enjoying the luxury of complete repose.

Toward evening he began to be a little uneasy, but with the dewy twilight, came Schio, waking the mysterious echoes, with his ringing laughter, and, as the darkness deepened, he placed a lantern in Joza's hand, saying: "Now, brother, we will go to the task you complain of so bitterly."

Silently they pursued their way, until they arrived at the huge pile, upon which the padre had appointed Joza to begin his work.

Many days would have passed before he could have hewn the rock as the padre desired, but, with one blow of an immense drill, in Schio's powerful hand, the rock was cleft in twain. As he reduced it to its proper size and shape, Joza stood by, trembling with fear; then pointed out the chosen spot, and, in silence and darkness, the first stone of the Grand San Pedro was laid.

When the full moon arose, clear and bright, shedding its floods of golden light over the mission of Santa Barbara, and the blue waves that washed its sanded shore, the laborers had gone—Joza, to sleep

7

peacefully in his little cottage, and Schio,
down to the echoing caverns by the sounding sea.

Morning came, gorgeous with sunshine
and beauty, and the padre walked out to
inspect the site of his ambitious dreams.

He was an avaricious and unscrupulous
man.

In building this new church, he hoped
to erect a tower of strength and greatness
for himself, more than an edifice in which to
worship the blessed Christ, the immaculate
Virgin, and the holy saints.

When he saw the huge foundation-stone
that Schio had laid, he was greatly amazed.

Even the hewing of it, he knew to be
the work of days, and there it was, cleanly
cleft, and in its proper place.

"There is a mystery here," he said ; " the
people will believe it a miracle; be it as it
will, I must make the most of it."

He called Joza, who came to him smiling and happy.

" You have done well for the beginning," said the padre, but to night, you must lay two stones like this."

" Holy San Pedro, help me!" exclaimed Joza. " It is impossible!" and he turned away, very sorrowful.

At night he told Schio what the padre had said. " Schio frowned, and answered, "The padre should not ask too much; but this shall be as he desires."

Again they went out in the twilight, and before the rising of the golden moon, two more foundation-stones were laid.

At daybreak the padre arose, and hastened to see if the task had been accomplished, and before his wondering eyes, lay the three immense foundation-stones, smooth, and in their proper places.

" Holy Virgin! I will give him enough

to-night," exclaimed the amazed padre, and again the task was doubled.

Thus it went on, night after night, and week after week, till the Grand San Pedro began to rise up like Aladdin's wonderful palace, but, Schio, the man of iron, grew very angry, as the full moon arose upon him, bending over his unfinished task.

"Joza," said he, "the padre may go too far for even Schio to bear; bid him be-ware!

"If the morning sun finds me here, I will not answer for the result; too much pressure will burst open the hidden recesses of earth, and cause the caverns of ocean to resound with fearful echoes of mystery.

"Can he think San Pedro will bless avarice and oppression, even in the padre Antonio?"

In the morning Joza went to the padre, and entreated him to lessen the task, but

he only laughed, and said: "You are getting fat and lazy. I will not double your
work to-night, but you shall do four times
as much as ever, and I will be there to see
it accomplished."

Joza departed with a heavy heart, dread-
ing to meet Schio; and when he told him
in the evening, he made no reply, but a
black frown covered his whole face, and his
eyes shot fire.

That night the padre Antonio went
out to watch Joza, and when he saw
Schio cleaving the huge stones with
one blow of his wonderful drill, he
thought he had not imposed task enough,
and resolved he would command him
to finish the Grand San Pedro in one
night.

Just after midnight the moon arose, and
the startled Joza heard, at every blow of
the drill, a hundred echoes ring out from

the ocean caverns. But Schio worked steadily on.

"Schio," said Joza, suddenly, "what is it makes these mournings from the sea caves?" But Schio only answered by a heavier blow from his hammer, and under their feet the ground shook violently, then opened, and, where the Grand San Pedro should have stood, yawned a great gulf, that closed upon the labor of many nights; and with the great foundation-stones went down the ambitious padre.

The morning sun rose on a scene of great desolation, but only Joza was there, with trembling voice, to tell the tale of the padre Antonio and the Grand San Pedro.

When others spoke of the great earth quake, he said: "'Twas all Schio's doings.

"The padre would never be satisfied, and the man of iron grew so angry, that he struck the great stone from the heart of the mountain, and then the earth shook, opened, and swallowed up the padre Antonio and the Grand San Pedro."

Schio was never afterward seen at the mission of Santa Barbara, but often, at evening, his ringing voice was wafted along the shore, from the cave of echoes, down by the sea.

In a small village upon the shore of the German Ocean lived a man whose wife had golden tresses so long and heavy that when they were unbound they covered her like a cloak of sunbeams, and reached to her feet. Her complexion was so fair, and her eyes so beautiful, that her equal was not to be found in all the Fatherland.

At last she fell sick and died, leaving her husband all alone in the world, except one wee baby, who lay sleeping in the cradle. At first the father was heart-broken, and noticed nothing, but after a time all his love turned to the helpless infant, who every day grew more lovely, and at last became as fair as her mother, with the same wealth of golden hair and soft violet eyes, and all the Fatherland, from far and near, was filled with the story of her great beauty.

When she was only a little maid, she would go down to the sea-shore and dance upon the sand, until her light straw hat would drop from her head, and her waving tresses fall about her like a shower of pure gold, and her violet eyes beam with the brightness of stars, while the flush upon her cheeks rivaled the soft, fresh bloom of the peach.

The maiden was called the fair Jung-frau Maleen, as she grew older and every day added to her charms, till half the young men in the country were ready to lay down their life for her; but though her ways were winning, and she had a pleasant smile for all, no one could be

7*

familiar with her. In her guileless innocence and beauty she seemed a great way
out of their reach, yet she danced with
them, talked and laughed with them, till
her clear, sweet voice rang out upon the
air like the soft notes of a silver bell, but
when she turned away, they felt that she
had gone from them forever.

Among her lovers was a bashful student
named Handsel, who worshiped the Jung-
frau Maleen with all the devotion of his
great noble heart, but ever at a distance.

He seldom spoke to her.

Even the rustle of her dress as she passed
along would set his heart to beating
wildly, and the sound of her voice, or one
glance of her violet eye would send the
hot blood rushing through his veins, dyeing
his face and neck a deep crimson. Poor
Handsel!

He would say to his heart, "Down, fool,

the star of heaven is not for you, look for some lovely flower of earth," but in all the Fatherland he knew there was not another maiden who could satisfy the hunger of his heart.

At all the village festivals he looked on in the distance, and saw others worship at the shrine he dared not approach. " I have nothing worth offering her," he would say, and so he was silent.

He was handsome and manly, and Maleen always looked for him in the crowd, and when she saw him standing far apart with his large dark eyes fixed upon her, she was more content than in his absence. If she had questioned her heart for the reason of this she would have blushed with confusion, for Jung-frau Maleen was not one who would willingly yield her heart unsought.

Maleen always loved the bright, sparkling sea, and often she would go out alone in her little boat, and sail for hours over the blue waters, gathering the pretty sea-weed, and indulging in the day-dreams that German maidens love.

One morning as Handsel was going to the college, he saw the Jung-frau step into her boat and push away from the shore.

He took off his hat and bowed.

She looked at him with that rare, sweet smile that always made him happy for days.

He stopped and looked back after her as the boat glided from the shore, and it seemed as though the sunshine of heaven and its bright reflection upon the waters were united, and was poured out in one rich flood of glory over her golden hair.

Handsel passed on out of the light into the quiet seclusion of the college, and bending over his book did not notice the rising of a thick, black cloud that from a

tiny speck soon swept over the whole sky,
then burst into wind and rain.

He was living over the heroic ages of the
olden time, when the darkness fell across his
book, and looking out the window he saw
the fierce storm gathering, and heard the
wailing winds crying out, Maleen! Maleen!
'Twas but the work of a moment to rush
out into the storm and down to the lashed
sea-shore and there, he saw a crowd of
anxious faces all turned hopelessly out
upon the pitiless breakers.

He looked, and there tossed wildly upon
the white-capped waves, rose and fell the
frail boat, and pale and hopeless sat the
pride of the Fatherland, the beautiful
Jung-frau Maleen, her matchless golden
hair hanging like a damp shroud about
her.

There were the hosts of her admirers
standing upon the shore wringing their

hands and weeping, they saw only death in an attempt to save her, and no one was so mad as to venture out upon the storm-lashed sea.

Even her father stood paralyzed in the hopelessness of his agony.

A strong, manly voice burst in upon the echoes of the storm. "A boat! a boat!" cried Handsel, with a stout-hearted determination in his voice to brave the danger of the breakers, and save the maiden he loved from the angry waters.

A long rope was tied about his body, and in a moment more the life-boat was tossing upon the crested waves, with the brave student at the prow, and the poor helpless Maleen rose up and held out her white arms toward him.

On over the cruel waves, the boats were nearing each other. The agony of suspense that filled the breathless crowd!

Great God! if they should meet and crash together!

Down they went into the great sea gulf; Maleen with outstretched arms, and Handsel with his great heart beating like a signal-drum in his bosom, pale but unfaltering.

Down! down they went!

Now up came the billow, but only one boat, and Handsel at the prow was struggling for the shore.

"Oh, Maleen! Maleen!" burst from the father's white lips, then a tress of rich golden hair hanging over the side of the boat met his sight, and he knew that Maleen was in the boat with Handsel.

On it came to the shore, like a charmed boat it escaped the perilous breakers, till at last, no one could tell how, only through God's great mercy, they were saved, and Handsel stood upon the shore with Maleen in his arms.

He gave the maiden to her weeping father, then sank away, and no one thought of him, all were gathered around Maleen, who had fainted.

Soon she opened her violet eyes, and looked around searchingly through the crowd with a strange fear. " Where, where, is Handsel ?" she cried, in wild excitement.

Then they all wondered how they could have forgotten him, and looking round they saw him sitting alone, with his head bowed down upon his hands. He did not want their thanks.

'Twas joy enough to him, that he had saved Maleen, and, brave man as he was, he sat there weeping like a child.

Maleen rose up, and walked feebly to him, and kneeling down upon the sand, she put her hand upon his shoulder, and whis-pered " Handsel !"

Handsel raised his head, and saw what

he had never dared hope for, in the soft voilet eyes upturned to his.

He answered only, "Maleen!" and, throwing his arms around her, pressed her fair golden-crowned head to his bosom.

Thus it was, that in the presence of God, the storm, and all the people—there by the the wild sea-shore, Handsel was betrothed to the most beautiful maiden in all the dear Fatherland,—The Jung-frau Maleen.

JUANETTA;

OR,

THE TREASURE OF THE LAKE OF THE TULIES.

A GREAT many years ago, before the discovery of the wonderful gold mines of California, there lived in Los Angelos an old
Spanish family of pure Castilian blood.

Don Carlos De Strada was very rich.
Far as the eye could reach his broad acres
were spread out to his admiring view, and
his flocks and herds almost literally fed
upon a thousand hills.

His house was large and commodious,
built after the Spanish fashion—an adobe
house—surrounded on all sides by a wide
piazza, and in the center an open court-

yard. The windows were guarded by latticed bars of iron, and all the gates and
doors were opened by massive keys. Bolts
and bars belong as much to a Spanish
house, as light elegancies to the hotel of a
Parisian.

When Don Carlos left the banks of the
Guadalquivir for the wild Lake of the Tulies, he brought with him a beautiful young
wife, who loved him with all the passion-
ate ardor of a Spanish woman.

It was a great change for the dainty
lady, from the stately halls of castellated
Spain to the wilderness of Los Angelos,
although it was a wilderness of sweets, and
the most enchanting climate in the world.
Though the Don was a thorough-bred aris-
tocrat, he was a shrewd business man, and
so intent was he on becoming a great lord
of the soil in the new country, that he did
not notice the roses fading from the olive

cheeks of his wife, and the soft mellow light of the woman's eye giving place to the more ethereal brightness of spiritual fire.

Spanish women seldom work, but in their hours of apparent listlessness they indulge in wild and ardent imaginings; and thus she would sit on the vine-clad piazza of the inner court, looking up to the clear sky, unrivaled even in Italy, until she would almost fancy, from the heavens above, she heard the rippling of the blue waters of the Guadalquivir.

There was one great hunger of her heart the Don seldom satisfied. She was his wife, and beautiful; as such, he loved her; but he never lavished the thousand little endearments upon her that is the natural food of woman's heart.

As the evening drew near, she would go to the barred window and look out upon the luxurious landscape, thinking only of

the coming of her lord; and when she saw
him, she would go timidly out to meet him,
and hold her beautiful oval face up for a
kiss, longing for him to throw his arms
around her, and, if only for a moment, hold
her to his heart.

He would kiss her lightly, saying, cold-
ly: "There, that will do; be a woman
now, not a baby." Then she would call
up a quiet dignity, until she could steal for
a few moments away, unobserved, and press
her hands tightly upon her heart, saying:
"If he would only love me! If he would
only love me, I could live away from home,
away from Spain, from every thing, for him!
I must learn to be a woman, and then, at
least he'll respect me.

"Oh, dear! I wish he didn't think it
so foolish in me to want to be loved! But
I must go to him. I'll try and talk like a
woman, but I don't know any thing about

the business that occupies his thoughts and time. He never tells me any thing because he thinks I'm such a baby. If he'd only love me, and let me be a baby sometimes, I think I'd be more of a woman."

Then the young wife would try to call up from her weakness new strength, and wiping away the traces of her emotion, would go out to be what pleased her lord, only a little paler, but with heart-strings quivering like an Æolian harp in a cold north wind.

One year passed in the strange, new country, and a beautiful babe was born to the ancient house of De Strada, but the mother died, and was buried by the clear Lake of the Tulies.

Don Carlos wept for his beautiful young wife, whose heart had been a sealed book, "Love, the Secret of Happiness," written for him in an unknown tongue.

His days of mourning were few. The rain fell upon the new-made grave as he gave the infant in charge of an Indian nurse who had just lost her own little baby. The savage mother took the child to her bosom, while the polished father turned away and looked out upon the green hills rich in verdure, counting the probable increase of his flocks and herds in the coming year, and, in the pleasant prospect, forgot his sorrow.

The little Juanetta grew to be a beautiful, healthy child, under the care of her indulgent nurse.

She knew where all the wild flowers grew, could shoot an arrow very well, or climb a tree, and, in many of the curious arts of the tribe, was quite skillful.

She was well versed in all the Indian traditions, and believed them with childish credulity. She seemed to have drawn the wildness of the Indian nature from the dusky bosom of her nurse, and with her little bow and arrow would roam the woods for whole days.

At times her father would ask the nurse, " How is Juanetta?" and, at the reply, " The child is well," he would forget that every day she was growing less and less an infant, and needed more and more a mother's care.

Thus things went on until she was eleven years old. She was very tall of her age, with her long black hair hanging over her graceful shoulders, her rich olive complex-ion deepened by the glowing sun, and her dark eyes, fawn-like in their softness and timidity, she looked like a beautiful child of the wild wood.

Her father would look at her, and say : " The girl is a perfect savage ; she must be placed at a convent ; the Sisters would soon make a lady of her, for the De Strada blood is rich in her veins;" and then he would smile proudly at her rare beauty.

The summer following brought a change to Don Carlos. Till then he had been prosperous; but there had been no rain, and the grass withered and dried up until the famished cattle died by thousands, and the hills, once covered with animal life, were left bare and desolate. Don Carlos, who lost heavily, became more than ever absorbed in business cares, and again the child was forgotten.

Juanetta saw that her father was greatly troubled, and she thought if she could only find some of the treasures hidden so many years ago by the great Chief of the Tulies, she could make him rich again, and he would smile upon her as he sometimes used to before the cattle died—since then, his dark frowning face had frightened her.

8

She had often listened to her old nurse, sitting by the clear lake, as she told her how, years ago, a great ship came to Los Angelos filled with fair men, with long flowing beards, golden in the sunshine, and eyes like the blue summer sky, and how there was one among them, taller and nobler than all the rest, who was their Chief.

For days they rode about the country, making their camp by the Lake of the Tulies, and tradition said they brought beautiful shining stones, that glistened like the stars of night, and great sacks of yellow gold to the lake, and buried them there at midnight; then went away in the great ship over the water.

They were seen by an old Indian woman, who was gathering magic herbs, but from that moment it seemed as though a fearful spell had fallen upon her, for when she tried to tell the story, just as she was about to speak of the place where the treasure was hidden, her tongue would cleave to the roof of her mouth, and she could not utter a word; and when she attempted to go to the spot where it was buried, her feet would fasten themselves to the ground, and she could not move. From that night she seemed bewitched, and she soon died, taking the secret of the buried treasure with her to the unknown spirit land.

Juanetta had nothing to do but listen to the wild Indian lore, and roam through the woods and down by the Lake of the Tulies; and it was not strange that with her poetic temperament, she reveled in the marvelous, till it seemed to her the natural and the real.

She longed for the magic talisman to point her to the hidden treasure, and show

her the wonders of the deep, until she felt
sure that one day she should discover it.
She told all these fancies to her nurse, who
was almost her only companion, and who
encouraged her, believing her, in her fond
love, to be one of the Great Spirit's chosen
children.

The winter came on with rare beauty.
The rain, so long withheld, fell copiously,
until the hills were covered with luxurious
verdure and gorgeous flowers. Don Carlos's
heart grew lighter; he might hope to recover his losses in time. The orange
orchard was laden with fruit, and the
lemons fell to the ground from the bending
trees. Juanetta loved the green grass, the
fragrant flowers, and the golden fruit, and
her wild nature expanded into the poetry
of the year.

One morning she rose with the crimson
dawning, and, stealing away while her old

nurse slept, she ran softly to the Lake of
the Tulies, and bathed her face in the clear
water till the brightness of youth and
morning seemed united in her radiant
beauty.

Suddenly Juanetta stopped, her tiny
hand dripping with water, half raised to
her glowing face, and her soft, dark eyes
sparkling with strange excitement. Upon
the brow of the distant hill, still covered
with the mist of the morning, she saw the
Chief of the Lake of the Tulies. She knew
it was him by the soft, purple light that
gathered around him; by the glow of perpetual youth that enveloped him, and by
the crimson clouds that dropped their
fleece so near, and yet could not conceal his
noble bearing.

To her eye, there seemed a shining glory
about his bronze beard, and his brow and
cheeks glowing in the early sunlight, were

fairer than any she had ever seen among the dusky Indian tribes or olive Spaniards.

Down the hill he came, a light straw hat in his hand, and the air playing with the light waves of his abundant hair. On he came to the lake, and to the spot where the little maiden sat, full of wonder and admiration.

He, too, seemed a little surprised when he saw her, but in the soft Spanish tongue, bade her "Good morning," and asked whose little girl she was, and what had brought her so early to the charmed lake.

"I am Don Carlos's daughter, Juanetta," said the child, "and you, the Chief of the Lake of the Tulies?"

A smile gathered around the lips of the Chief, and filled his blue eyes, with a light so pleasant that the child drew near him, and placed her little brown hand confidingly in his. He drew her to him, saying, kindly:—

"You know me, then? I am the Chief of the Lake of the Tulies, and what can I do for the little Juanetta?"

"Tell me," said the child, "of all the wonderful treasures hidden by the lake, and of the palaces of the sea, and the coral groves under the great waters!"

The Chief led her to a rock that overhung the lake, and told her to look over into the waters, and she saw them clear and sparkling in the morning sun, and it seemed as though the light of a thousand brilliants was stealing through the shining waves.

He told her of glittering diamonds beneath the sea, richer far than all the hills and valleys of Los Angelos, covered with flocks and herds; and how the coral trees outshone the trees of earth, in beauty, and of the crystal palaces of the deep, and of the maidens of the sea, whose purple hair like sea-weed, sometimes floated above the waves.

Juanetta told him she had often found locks of their silken hair upon the beach, and how beautiful it was. He told her of the sounding shells, and ocean harps breathing their rich, deep-toned melody, and the thousand mysteries of the wild sea lore, till the delighted Juanetta begged him to take her with him down, down to the crystal caves, and let her become a sea-maiden, and gather pearls under the blue waters of the deep.

But he replied: "You are a child of the woods, not of the wave; you may become an immortal spirit in the sky, but never in the deep, deep sea."

Tears gathered in her eyes, and she said: "You are cruel to Juanetta, Chief of the

Lake of the Tulies. You of all your
wealth of beauty, will grant Juanetta nothing. Juanetta must live alone, in the
woods and fields, with only the old nurse
and the father who always forgets her."

He soothed the little maiden gently, and
told her he would grant her greater treasures than those of the deep, if she would
obey him; and she kissed his hand and
promised.

Then he took from his bosom, a talisman,
and gave it to her, saying : "Juanetta, this
cross will guard you from evil spirits.
When you are troubled or angry, take it
from your bosom, and ask the great Father
above to bless you and help you. Do this
earnestly five minutes, and the evil spirits
will leave you." And Juanetta kissed the
cross and promised.

"I have yet another talisman" he continued, "and very powerful. It opens a new

8*

world of delight and beauty, to those who
are willing to give their time, care, and
diligent attention to the study of it.
Would you like it, Juanetta? You could
no longer wander all day through the .
woods, hunting wild-flowers, or dream
away your life by the Lake of the Tulies.
Could you give up the wild pleasures of
your present life, for the gifts of the talisman I have promised?"

Juanetta's face was glowing with wonder and delight; she longed to enter the
unknown promised land :

"I will do any thing, I will give up any
thing you tell me, she cried, with enthusi-
asm."

She was enchanted with the unseen gifts
that left so much to her fervid imagination
to picture, and she was delighted with the
giver, the handsome young Chief of the
Lake of the Tulies, whose pleasant smile,

and pleasing words, made morning's golden sunshine in her heart.

"But won't you show me where the treasure of the Lake of the Tulies lies hidden?" she said, blushingly. "All those rare gems, crimson, purple, golden, and diamonds sparkling like the morning dew. What can be more beautiful than these?"

All her life, Juanetta had heard of the matchless luster of these hidden jewels, and now to be so near them, with the Chief of the Lake of the Tulies by her side, she felt that her day dreams of beauty might, with one word of his, or a touch of his magic wand, be realized.

"Do not ask for too much in one morning, Juanetta," he replied, laughing. "Now for talisman number two," and he took a book from his pocket, and until the sun had risen high in the heavens, they sat bending over it together with mutual pleasure.

Then the Chief of the Lake of the Tulies arose, taking her little bronzed hand in his, saying: "I must go, my little Juanetta. Keep the talisman, and study it well. The new morning is dawning for you now; what a queen of light 'twill make you?" And he passed his hand over the thick waves of tangled hair that fell in long masses over the shoulders of the beautiful child.

Tears gathered in the dark eyes of the maiden. "Are you going now, Chief of the Lake of the Tulies?" said she, sadly: "Going to the crystal palaces of the sea? And shall you take the treasure of the lake with you? Take the talisman, I can do nothing without you! Here alone! Only the old nurse, and the father who never thinks, never thinks of Juanetta! And you, too, will forget Juanetta!"

"No! no, Juanetta, I will not forget you,

but will come again to-morrow. I will not go to the sea, since you cannot go, but will stay and teach you the use of the talisman, and the treasure of the lake shall rest till we can find it together! So now good-by to-day."

And then they parted, and Juanetta was very happy in the light of the new dawning.

All day long she studied, and many successive days, and the Chief of the Lake of the Tulies always came, either at morning or at evening, to hear her lesson.

Sometimes she would ask him about the hidden treasure, as they walked by the lake; he would smile and say, "I have found a treasure by the Lake of the Tulies richer than all the gems of the ocean," and when Juanetta begged him to show it to her, he would tell her to look into the water; but she could see only the reflection of her own sweet face, full of wondering happiness.

Then he would laugh again, and say, he could not tell her now of his treasure by the Lake of the Tulies, but he would describe the rich gold mine he had discovered in the cañon, and tell her there was gold enough in it almost to fill up the lake.

Thus weeks and months passed by. Juanetta was twelve years old. She had improved rapidly in her studies, and had learned to call her young teacher by another name, not so long or high sounding, but very pleasant to them both, and often they would laugh at their first strange meeting by the charmed Lake of the Tulies.

At last her father was aroused to the sense of her increasing beauty. He saw, that the years of childhood were fast passing away, and that she stood upon the threshold of dawning womanhood.

He was greatly surprised, and delighted to find her proficient in studies of which he supposed she knew nothing, and he made all possible haste to have her placed at a convent, where she could enjoy every advantage of culture and refinement.

The young stranger who had been her teacher, became a great favorite with Don Carlos. He was engaged in developing a mine, in the San Francisco cañon, in which he succeeded in amassing great wealth, though in after years the mine failed to yield its store of golden treasure.

Four years passed away, and Juanetta returned to her father's house, an accomplished, and beautiful lady. Again by the Lake of the Tulies, she met the Chief of her childhood's dreams, and there together, they found the treasure greater than all the wealth of land or sea, the pure and earnest love of their youthful hearts.

They were married, and Don Carlos's
heart swelled proudly, as he thought of the
great wealth their union had brought into
his family, while they blessed God for the
lifelong treasure He had given them, by
the charmed Lake of the Tulies.

ONCE upon a time there lived near a small village on the shore of the Atlantic, an honest farmer named Norton, who had three sons.

The two elder were smart, active lads, but the youngest was quiet, and so much given to dreaming that his brothers ridiculed and often slighted him.

"He is so stupid," they would say, "he will be a disgrace to the family;" but what annoyed him most, they gave him the unpleasant *sobriquet* of Dumpy, on account of his fat, rosy cheeks.

As the boys grew up, the eldest took the farm, and was to take care of the father and mother, the second became clerk to a merchant in a neighboring city, but poor Dumpy, in the indolence of his disposition, did nothing. He was always hoping some impossible thing would " turn up," but he had no rich relations, indeed no one seemed to take much interest in him but the mother, who would always say, " Poor Dumpy, he is a good-hearted boy," then she would sigh heavily, as though there was nothing more to be said.

At last the father became quite out of patience, and calling the boy to him one day, he said: " You are now twenty years old, and never have earned so much as your salt, and it is quite time for you to do something for yourself. Your brother, who has taken the farm, complains that he is obliged to support you in idleness, which certainly is not right."

" For the farm he will take care of your

mother and me, but you and your other brother must look out for yourselves."

"Give me," answered Dumpy, "what money you can spare, I ask nothing more, I will go and seek my fortune, and you shall hear of me when I become a rich man."

The father gave him what money he could, and he went away, no one at home knew whither, leaving only the mother to weep for him.

When Dumpy left the farm-house he walked on to the village, feeling that he was going into the great world full of promise, but he never dreamed of disappointment.

When he arrived at the village inn the stage was standing at the door. "I will go," he said, "where fortune leads me." So he took his seat in the stage, and paid his fare to the end of the route, which happened to be the great city of New York.

All day long he was very happy looking
out of the windows upon the changing
landscape, and indulging in day-dreams.
Sometimes he would come to a pretty village nestling among the hills. "I would
like," he would think, "of all things to stop
here, 'tis so very pleasant, but I have paid
my money, and I must go on."

It was night when the stage entered the
city, its heavy wheels rumbling over the
paved streets, and crowding along past carts,
omnibuses, and carriages, till poor Dumpy,
who had never been in the city before,
began to feel very much bewildered and
confused.

"Where shall I go," said Dumpy to the
driver, when the stage stopped. "'Tis so
noisy I can't hear myself think. Oh, dear!
I don't know what to do," and he looked so
pitiably helpless that the driver was sorry
for him, though he could not help laugh-

ing. "Come with me, my boy," he said, so he went with the driver to the cheap lodging-house, where he stopped when in town.

To enumerate all poor Dumpy's adventures while in New York would be impossible. Enough to say it was not long before his money was gone, and he shipped before the mast in a merchant vessel for California.

Poor Dumpy! Now came woful experiences, for a time he was wretchedly seasick, and he soon found that to go before the mast was no joke, but in his way he was quite a philosopher, and after a few weeks became a very good sailor.

As he was pleasant and obliging he became a favorite with all on board, but he loved most of all when off duty, to sit by himself in the soft starlit evenings as the good ship sailed over the tropic seas, and dream of the land of gold to which he was going.

He possessed a vivid imagination, and his visions of the wealth of the new Eldorado were most glowing.

He would picture to himself how like a prince he would luxuriate in riches, how great and generous he would be, even to the brothers who had despised him. It is a happiness to be able to revel in dreams as he did, for the pleasures of anticipation are but too often greater than the reality.

He loved his mother, she at least had always been kind and gentle to him.

"My dear mother," he would say to himself, with a bright tear in his eye, "she shall yet live in a palace. God bless her, dear mother."

Then he would sigh till a bright thought drove away the sad one. "Oh, 'tis so delightful to be rich," he would say.

Then he would rub his hands as complacently as though the wealth of the Indies lay at his feet.

"I shall give the father every thing he wishes of course," he would continue, "and I will make the brothers rich men, for to be generous and forgive is the attribute of true greatness, and for myself I will marry the prettiest woman in the world, and I will give her every thing she can possibly desire."

Often the sharp quick bell, for change of watch, would call him to duty, and scatter his gorgeous dreams, leaving only the dull, hard present in his mind and heart.

At length the good ship arrived in San Francisco, and there again Dumpy found all the wild bustle and confusion of the early days.

Gold was plenty in dust and bars.

When a man bought any thing he would

take out of his bag of gold dust as much dust as he was to pay for the article, and he would be off.

The highest price was paid for labor, and Dumpy soon engaged to drive a cart for two hundred and fifty dollars per month, but he determined to make this arrangement only for a short time, till he could get money enough to go out prospecting in the mining districts.

This he soon accomplished, but he found a life in the mines even harder than before the mast, but the golden future was before him, and he persevered.

He and another young adventurer built a cabin together by a little spring of clear, bubbling water.

They worked early and late, with the wearisome pick and shovel for the precious gold that was to pave the pathway of their lives with happiness, but often night found them disappointed and weary, and they would return to their lonely cabins, cook and eat their coarse supper, and lie down upon the hard floor, wrap their blankets around them, with heavy and hopeless hearts. But thank God, sunshine and the fresh morning brings renewed life and hope to young hearts.

One morning when Dumpy awoke he found his companion had risen and gone out before him, so he went out alone, thinking, "who knows what will turn up before night, I may become a millionaire. I'll try my luck alone to-day;" so he did not go to the ledge they had been prospecting the day before, but started off in a new direction.

All day long he worked diligently, but the sunset found him as poor as the dawning, and quite worn out, he threw himself down upon the ledge to rest a little before

9

going home. "Ah, me!" thought he, sadly, how long the poor mother will have to wait for her palace."

As the sunset deepened into twilight, he rose, and shouldering his pick and shovel, started for the cabin. "I can not call it home," he said to himself, "there is no mother there."

He had not gone far, before a little shrill voice arrested him, and looking down, he saw a little old man, sitting among the loose stones, rubbing his foot and ankle, and groaning piteously.

He was very quaintly dressed, in a little red jacket, and wore a Spanish hat with little gold bells around it, and his long gray beard swept the ground, as he sat dismally among the rocks.

"Oh, dear! I cannot move," said the little man; "I have sprained my foot, will not you help me home? Oh dear! oh dear!" and he moaned so piteously that Dumpy, who was kind-hearted, was very sorry for him; so he took the old man up in his arms as tenderly as if he had been an infant.

The old man pointed out the way, and Dumpy trudged wearily on, for though he was no bigger than a child of eight years old, he seemed quite heavy to Dumpy. After working all day with the pick and shovel, and finding nothing, his heart was heavy with hope deferred. "If I had found gold to-day," thought he, "a light heart would have made a light burden; but thank God I am well, and this poor man suffers fearfully."

Poor Dumpy! He went on, down the cañon, then up the mountain, it seemed to him for miles; at last the little man pointed to a crevice in the rock, through which Dumpy managed with some difficulty to creep; but as he went on it widened, and suddenly opened into a large cavern.

"Go on," said the old man, sharply, as Dumpy stopped and gazed around with astonishment. So he went on till they came to a large hall sparkling with crystal, and glowing with precious stones.

A large chandelier hung from the roof, and cast a flood of softened light through the whole cavern, and Dumpy could see in the stone floor large masses of pure yellow gold.

He saw in the huge irregular pillars that rose to the dome of the cavern, great veins of the precious ore, and everywhere it was scattered about with the most lavish profusion.

Curious golden figures, carved with strange devices, stood in the niches, and there were couches with golden frames, and tables of gold, so that the light, reflected from the clear crystal dome, glittering with shining pendants, by the softening yellow tinge, was mellow and pleasant.

Poor Dumpy had been so long in the twilight and darkness, that he was dazzled by the brilliant scene, and for a few moments was obliged to close his eyes, and when he opened them, he saw that he was surrounded by a large crowd of the little people, who were full of anxious fears about the old man he held in his arms, but he assured them he was suffering only from a sprain, which, though very painful, was not dangerous. They gathered anxiously around the little man as he laid him upon a couch.

He soon discovered that the man he had assisted was king over the little people who guard the mountain treasures, covering the rich places with unpromising stones

and earth, and often misleading the honest
miner by scattering grains of the precious
metal in waste places; thus it is we hear so
often of disappointed hopes, and abandoned
mines.

After they had in some measure relieved
the suffering of their chief, they turned to
Dumpy, who stood in the most profound astonishment, drinking in all he saw or heard.

"You have done me a great kindness,"
said the chief; "and, though it is our business to mislead miners, we can be grateful,
and you may now claim any reward you
desire."

"I have saved your ruler," said Dumpy,
looking at the crowd of little people, and
trying to think of something great to ask
as a reward.

"Our chief! our king!" cried all the little people, together. "Ask what you will
and it shall be granted."

"I would be great as well as rich," thought Dumpy, so he said aloud: "Make me emperor of all the mines, and let all the miners pay tribute to me."

"It shall be so," said the king. Then he called one of his servants to bring the golden crown and scepter, and bidding Dumpy kneel before him, he placed the scepter in his hand and the crown upon his head, and striking him a sharp blow upon his shoulder, he said, "Arise, Emperor Norton.

"As long as you preserve this crown and scepter from moth or rust, dew or fog, you shall be the true emperor of all the mines in California and Nevada, and all the miners shall pay you yearly tribute, but if you lose either crown or scepter, or moth, rust, midnight dews and damps fall upon them, they will fade away, and you will be emperor in name

only, and the miners shall pay you no
yearly tribute."

"So let it be," said the newly-made emperor; and they all sat down to a table
spread with every delicacy, and feasted till
the noon of the following day.

When the emperor bade the knights of
the mountain adieu, the little gray king
said: "Beware of the dews and damps of
the night," and he started for his cabin.

"I will first visit my old comrade," he
said, "though he is now one of my subjects,
I will not be proud and haughty."

One of the little men ran before him, and
led the way out of the cave into the sunlight, which was so bright that the emperor shaded his eyes with his hand, and
when he had removed it the little man had
disappeared.

The emperor looked around, but could
see no trace of him; even the crevice

through which he had passed, was no-
where to be seen.

"It is a wonderful dream," said he; but
no! there was the golden crown upon his
head, and the scepter in his hand.

"I will find that cave," thought he; so
he began to look for it very eagerly, till the
lengthening shadows told of the coming of
evening, and he thought of the gray king's
warning, " Beware of the dews and damps
of night."

"Oh dear! if I should lose the tribute
money," he said, in great distress; "I
should be emperor but could build no palace for the mother, nor could I marry the
prettiest woman in the world, and supply
her innumerable wants;" so he started in
great haste for the camp, always keeping
fast hold of the crown and scepter.

On he rushed till the shades of twilight
filled the deep cañon, through which he

9*

was obliged to pass, then he broke into a run, crying, "Oh me! if I should be too late! too late! now that my hopes are crowned with success. Too late! too late!"

"Haste makes waste," and so the emperor found it. He lost the path and became entangled in brush and rocks, until he became almost wild with despair.

The night came on with a heavy mist that near morning deepened into rain.

With the gray twilight of the dawning, weary and worn, he reached his cabin door, but the golden crown and scepter had passed away into the mists of night.

The poor emperor told of his wanderings to his comrades, and mourned over the night in which his crown and scepter had departed from him, but they only laughed, saying, "You have been dreaming again, Emperor Norton."

"He never took the pick and shovel

again. "Shall an emperor work," he would say, "while thousands of his subjects roll in luxury?"

An emperor, he thought, should reside in the chief city of his realm, so he left the mines and came to San Francisco.

Here for years he has lived, always wearing a well-worn suit of blue, with epaulettes upon the shoulders, which, perhaps, might have been an unmentioned gift of the gray king of the mountains.

At the table of all restaurants and hotels he is a free and welcome guest, and all places of amusement are open to him; in fact, wherever you go in San Francisco, you are almost sure to meet the Emperor Norton.

DEATH'S VALLEY;

OR,

THE GOLDEN BOULDER.

YEARS ago, even before what Californians understand to be the "early days," Dick Fielding was promoted to a captaincy in the United States Army.

Merry days were those, while he was stationed near the metropolitan city. Good pay, little work, brilliant parties to attend, and beautiful women to make love to. Love making seemed the natural element of the gay young captain, and thanks to his handsome face and shining epaulettes, he was very successful.

In this world our dear delights are but
fleeting as the smiles of an April day—so
thought poor Dick as he sat one morning
about eleven o'clock at his luxurious breakfast, reading a dispatch from head-quarters
that doomed him to the wilderness of Fort
Tejon, far below the quaint old Spanish
town of Los Angelos.

'Twas a sad day for the gallant young
captain, but all his sighs and regrets were
unavailing. There was no reprieve—
orders must be obeyed. Fortunately Dick
was of an elastic temperament, and the love
of adventure and the charm of novelty
which the new country possessed for him
soon returned to him that zest for life
which youth and health seldom entirely
lose.

Southern California has a most generous
climate, producing in the valleys the luxurious vegetation of the tropics, and on the

hills and mountains the hardier products of the temperate zone.

Dick was a favorite among the officers, social and joyous in his disposition, he became the life of the garrison. He was a fine horseman, and often he would join a party of the Mexican rangers in their excursions, and ride for days over the beautiful country round Fort Tejon.

He could shoot an arrow very handsomely, and by his easy good nature he was soon on friendly terms with the Indians, who in that part of the country are so mixed with the native Californians or Mexicans that it is difficult to distinguish the races.

He became an expert in all the athletic sports of the country, but with all he could do, the monotony of a life at Fort Tejon was very wearisome to him; so when he found a beautiful young girl among the

Indians, he plunged recklessly into his old habit, of love making; and in a few weeks he was domesticated in a little adobe house near the fort with his pretty Indian bride, who amused him for the time like any other novelty of the country.

She, poor simple child of the wildwood, worshiped her handsome, blue-eyed husband, and thought his hair and beard had stolen their golden beauty from the glowing sunshine.

After a time a little one came to the cottage, and the young Indian mother was very happy in loving the father and child who made the wilderness a heaven for her.

Weeks, months, and years passed by, and Captain Fielding longed intensely to visit the gay world again. He had grown weary of his Indian wife, and his son in his eyes was only a young papoose, of whom he was very much ashamed.

At length the order came for his reprieve. He was summoned to return to the Atlantic States; but of this he said nothing to his wife. One bright spring morning he left her looking out after him from the door of the little adobe, holding her three-year old boy in her arms, smiling and telling him in her own soft language that dear papa would come back at evening.

The burning fingers of remorse pressed heavily upon the father's heart as he looked upon the pretty picture—but only for a moment. He turned away, saying with a sigh of relief: "She'll soon forget me, for some Indian Chief, perhaps," and was gone from her sight out into the distance, on toward the great busy world.

Night came on with its damps and darkness, wrapping the heart of the young wife in its shroud of shadows, never to be lifted till the brightness of the spirit land made glad morning shine about her.

Day by day she watched the shadows lengthen, hoping when the sun went down in the crimson west he would return; but the golden moonlight found her watching in vain, swaying her sleeping boy too and fro in her arms, and drearily singing the song of her heart, in a voice from which the gladness of hope was fast dying out.

She called him Dick, for his father, and with a perseverance which only deep love could give her, talked his father's language to him in her pretty, imperfect way.

The little one grew to be a strong, hand-some boy, with a dark Spanish face, and eyes full of fire, or love as his mood moved them. In some things he was like his father; gay, dashing, and attractive in his disposition, he became a great favorite with the officers at Fort Tejon, who taught him to read and write and many other things, much to the delight of his mother, who would say with tears in her dark eyes: "If his father lives to return he will thank you better than I can."

In the spring she would say: "Before the orange-flowers ripen to golden fruit he will return," and in the autumn, "before the fair buds gladen the green hillsides he will be here!"

But springs and autumns passed, till the broken spirit, hopeless and weary with waiting, passed into the unknown future, and they buried her where the first rays of the morning sun fell upon the graveyard flowers.

Dick loved his mother fondly, and after she died he grew more wild and daring than ever, but with the undercurrent of his nature flowed all the subtle instinct of the Indian.

Often at Fort Tejon he heard of the

great world far beyond the wilderness, and he learned that gold was the talisman that opened the gates of earthly paradise. So he said in his heart, "I will have gold!"

Young as he was and wild in his nature, he saw a witching paradise in the soft blue eyes and sunny curls of the Colonel's young daughter Madeline, but no one knew that he worshiped her, no one but God and his own heart.

Among the Indian and Spanish boys Dick was chief. To the lowliest he was gentle, to the proudest, superior, and by a wonderful magnetic power in one so young he bowed them all to his will. No one among them thought to question his bidding; he was the ruler, and without a thought they obeyed him. He could ride fearlessly the wildest horse, send the truest arrow from the bow, and laughed carelessly at danger as though he bore a charmed life.

One evening he lay upon the green grass before an Indian encampment, looking dreamily up at the great golden moon as it sailed along through the clear summer sky, surrounded by the paler light of the modest stars, and thinking how Madeline was like the moon, queen of all maidens.

The rest were beautiful, but in comparison with the sweet Madeline were but attendant lights. Then he thought of the great world where one day Madeline would shine fairest of the fair, and that before he could enter the charmed circle he must win the talisman that would give him every thing, but best of all, sweet Madeline.

Near him the Indian youths and maidens had gathered round an old man of their tribe, who was telling them the legend of the " Golden Boulder."

" Yes," said the old man, " white men would risk their lives for it, if they could only find the valley, but even the Indians except one tribe who make war upon all others, have lost trace of it; but there in the center rises a great round boulder, yellow as the full moon, all gold, pure gold!"

"Where?" cried Dick, springing with one bound into the circle. Then for the first time he listened to the old tradition of the Golden Boulder in Death's Valley.

"Far to the south," said the old Indian, "lies a country rich in gold and precious stones. The tribe who inhabits that region makes war with all who dare to cross the boundaries of their hunting-grounds. In some way they have become possessed of guns from which they shoot golden bullets with unerring precision.

"The country is shut in by mountains, and the great Colorado pours its waters through it. Far into the interior, deep down in the shadows, lies Death's Valley, and in its center rises the great Golden Boulder, and round it are scattered innumerable precious stones, whose brightness pierces the dusky shadows with their shining light."

The tradition came from an old man of the hostile tribe who many years ago was taken prisoner. Many adventurous Mexicans and Spaniards had sought Death's Valley, but none had ever returned from its shroud of shadows.

Dick listened to the story with deep attention. For days the thought of it pursued him, and at night when he closed his eyes the great round boulder of gold rose before him, and the glittering stones made the night shining as the day.

He could learn nothing more from the Indians than the old tradition, but every day he became more resolved, at any hazard, to win the great talisman, gold, which alone could open the door of happiness and greatness for him; even if he we reobliged to seek it among the shadows in Death's Valley, he would win it.

It was the early days of February, which in Lower California is the spring time of the year. Golden oranges still hung upon the trees amid the shining leaves and snow-white flowers, the buds of promise for the coming year, while everywhere gorgeous flowers brightened the fragrant hillsides and dewy valleys.

Without a word of farewell to any one, Dick started out into the trackless wilderness alone, with only his rifle and a small hatchet to blaze the trees now and then. Guided by the Indian's unerring instinct, he reached the Colorado, strong and vigorous as when he left the neighborhood of Fort Tejon.

He had wanted for nothing; his trusty

gun had supplied him with game, and the fruits of the wild-wood had furnished him dessert. Thus alone in the luxuriance of that sunny clime he wandered for days, but still no trace of the valley, or the Golden Boulder; but he was not disheartened.

Day and night, the gorgeous imagery that decked the future, gathered round him. As the reward of all this toil and lonely wanderings, he saw his golden hopes fulfilled, and the sunny curls of the Colonel's daughter resting upon his bosom. For this hope more than all others he labored on.

It was the close of an excessively hot day. The dewy coolness of evening was delightful to the weary gold-seeker, and he threw himself down upon his couch of leaves, under the shadow of the forest trees, thinking the way · was long and weary, and feeling the desolation of the solitary wilderness, casting its long shadows upon his heart.

But toil, is the mother of forgetfulness, and sleep was casting its drowsy mantle over his saddened musings, when his quick ear, detected a sound like a light, but rapid, footstep among the dried leaves. Nearer and nearer it came, snapping the brittle twigs that covered the ground.

He hastily concealed himself, and waited in almost breathless stillness the approach of wild beasts, or wilder Indians.

A moment more, and a young Indian girl appeared, bearing upon her head a birchen bucket. Light and graceful, with the freedom of the woods, she walked along until she came to a clear spring, and bending over, she filled her bucket with the pure fresh water.

Just then, a rare cluster of flowers attracted her eye, and with a maiden's love

10

of the beautiful, she stopped to gather it,
then poising her bucket upon her head,
she would have started for the encampment, but she was fastened spell-bound to
the spot, by an unconquerable terror.

Just opposite, and crouched ready to
spring upon her, she saw a huge panther,
his large eyes, like great balls of fire, glaring out from the intense shadow, already
devoured her. She was paralyzed by an
intense terror. The fearful eyes fascinated
and bewildered her. In them she saw the
frail bridge, that separated her from the
spirit land.

She could not move, or utter a sound.
The panther crouched lower among the
tangled grass. A moment more, and he
would spring upon her. The stream was
drawing nearer, the bridge was shorter,
from those fearful eyes, she could see the
gleaming of the lights of spirit land, then

a flash ! a sharp report of the rifle, and the panther sprang into the air, and fell at the feet of the affrighted maiden !

She lived ! but the waters of the spring were glowing red and warm with the lifeblood of the terrible beast. His glowing eyes grew dim and sightless, in the river of death, and in its place, to her sight appeared the handsome young gold-seeker.

With all her intense emotion, she was calm, as only an Indian maiden could be, but a deep glowing flush burned through the darkness of her cheek, as with timid grace, she gave her hand to her deliverer, and through the dusk of evening led him to the encampment, and to the chieftain, her father.

There was great excitement in the encampment when they saw the young girl returning with a stranger. Fiercely the

Indians of the hostile tribe gathered round them, for the girl clung tremblingly to his hand, and by the fitful firelight he saw the dark scowls of passion gathering upon their faces, yet a thrill of joy filled his heart, he now knew he was by the camp-fire of the wild tribe of whom nothing was known, save their uncompromising cruelty, and that with them rested the secret of Death's Valley, the great Golden Boulder, and the glittering stones.

He had saved their chieftain's daughter, and they would not harm him, for well he knew the power of gratitude upon the savage heart. Calm and resolute he stood among them, without the shadow of a fear darkening his face, until he saw the fierce fires of cruelty that shot from their wild eyes soften into the kindly light of gratitude and friendship, as the young girl told her story with all the pathos and ardor which the almost miraculous escape, had awakened in her heart.

The old chief loved his daughter with a savage intensity. She was all the Great Spirit had left him, of many sons and daughters, and he felt that he would be ready to battle with death itself, but he could not give up his only child.

There was a mist over his fierce eyes, and a trembling about his cruel heart, as he bade the stranger a kindly welcome, who but for his good fortune in saving the girl, would have been condemned to a torturing death, unheard of.

So it was at last by this unforeseen accident, that the young gold-seeker slept peacefully by the smouldering camp-fire of the most cruel, relentless, tribe of the Colorado, and dreamed of his blue-eyed darling, far away over the desert waste, safely sheltered in Fort Tejon.

The morning dawned rich with the
glowing warmth of a Southern climate,
and though our young hero woke early, he
was wearied from long travel, and lay for
some time with half-closed eyes, lazily
watching the Indians as they busied themselves about the encampment.

He was thinking how he should turn the
advantage he had gained to the furtherance
of his plans, when suddenly he felt, more
than saw, that dark, jealous eyes were
upon him. He feigned to be sleeping,
while by a stolen glance he understood
every thing.

The tall, stalwart, young Indian, who
bent over him with dark, knitted brows
and flashing eyes, loved the girl whom he
had saved, and was already his enemy,
and one not to be scorned, as his proud
bearing, and the deference shown him by
others attested. That he was in danger,

Dick realized; yet he rose with a free and careless manner, greeting the young men with a smile, which was returned.

"Worse than I supposed," he said to himself; "treachery! but they shall not find me unprepared!"

The old chief and his daughter treated him with marked kindness, and he, by his modesty and pleasantry, tried to make friends among the young men.

After breakfast preparations were made for a hunt, and Dick was furnished with a fresh horse, and invited to join the company.

The day was warm and sultry, and, toward evening, the hunters, in starting for the camp, became scattered, and, on entering the shadows of a deep ravine, Dick found himself surrounded by five of the strongest young men, and, prominent among them, his enemy.

In an instant of time his hands were pinioned, and he was ordered to prepare for death. Looking calmly upon the dark, scowling faces around him, he said: " I am ready, only I would make one request of Tolume (his enemy), 'tis this; that if in his wanderings he should ever reach Fort Tejon, he would bear a message for me to the woman I love."

The face of Tolume brightened, and he ordered the prisoner unbound, and leading him to a mossy stone, listened to the story of his love for the fair, blue-eyed maiden, of Fort Tejon, and of all his hopes and plans, till the sun went down and the silver moon looked into the ravine.

Tolume was jealous no longer; so they became friends, and after listening to the story of Death's Valley and the great Golden Boulder, he promised to go with Dick in search of it.

Nothing was said on their return to the camp of the closing event of the day's hunt, but Dick saw with great satisfaction, that his new friend and the dark-eyed girl he had saved from death, were again mutually happy.

Indians generally care but little for gold, but this tribe had mingled enough with the Spaniards to know something of its value; so the young Indian was very ready to accompany Dick in his adventures, and to accede to all his proposals, for he soon learned to look upon our hero as a superior being.

"To-night," whispered Dick, as he passed carelessly by the young Indian, "when the moon rises above the mountain-tops, we will start."

The Indian bowed assent, and looked fondly upon the young girl he must leave,

10*

and whom he loved with all the fierceness of his wild nature.

During the afternoon he told her he was going away for a short time, but would return bringing her beautiful feathers, embroidered moccasins, strings of shining beads, and all that the heart of a pretty Indian girl could desire. Then they parted, as all lovers part, with mingled hopes and fears.

When the moon rose clear and bright, casting its soft, mellow light over the glowing landscape, the young men met silently upon the brow of the hill, and started upon their journey.

They were well equipped with guns and ammunition. Each had a good horse, and as much food as they could carry ; the only thing they had to fear was lack of water and hostile Indians.

For two days they traveled on without

encountering any difficulty; but on the third they entered a dry, waste tract of country entirely destitute of vegetation.

The ground was covered with a formation of salt and soda, and when the wind blew it nearly suffocated them.

"This must be Death's Valley," said Dick, as they rode on, talking cheerfully, looking carefully for any signs of gold. By noon they began to feel very thirsty, but there was no water, no cooling spring in all the vast desert spread out before them.

The burning rays of the noontide sun seemed to dry up their blood, and their tongues were parched and feverish, but there was no shelter; no water. Heat, thirst, and travel began to tell upon their horses, so they dismounted, and led them by the bridle, till night came on, finding them weary and faint, and, above all, perishing with thirst. Their fevered tongues began to swell, and it seemed as though the salt dust permeated their whole bodies; but they dare not stop, even for a moment, they were dying of thirst, and there was no water.

At last the clear, full moon rose over the desert waste of Death's Valley and over the wayworn prospectors. They thought no more of gold, only of water—clear, cool, bubbling water.

It seemed to Dick as though he could hear the murmuring of the brook that rippled by the cottage of his childhood home, near Fort Tejon.

He walked along, every moment growing more hopeless, when suddenly he saw something bright and shining on the ground. It was a curious bow and quiver ornamented with little bells of silver and gold.

"Some one has been here, and only a short time ago, or the wind would have swept

away the track," said Dick, as he bent down
and examined a footprint upon the ground.
"'Tis too small for a man," he said. "'Tis
very strange."

Then he gave a loud shout, and they both
listened eagerly, till they heard a low faint
voice in reply, and, looking around, they
saw by the clear moonlight an odd little
figure trying in vain to rise from the
ground. The young men hastened to his
assistance, and found a queer, little dwarf,
with a long grey beard reaching nearly to
his feet.

"Give me water!" said the man. "My
horse has thrown me, and all day long I
have lain here in the burning sun, too weak
to move, for I am dying of thirst! Oh
give me water, only a drop of water!"

"No water! No water!" cried Dick, in
despair. "We, too, are famishing for want
of it! We must on, we have not a

moment to lose, or we shall die here in the desert."

"Do not leave me," cried the little man. "I can show you water, but I cannot move!" So they placed him upon one of the horses, and he pointed out the way.

Dick would have thrown aside the bow and quiver, but as he looked at the curious little being beside him, quaint old Indian traditions came to his mind.

"This bow may serve me yet," he said, as he secured it to his leather belt. "Who knows but it belongs to one of the dwarf treasure-guard of the valley."

All night they traveled on and till nearly noon the next day, when a little green spot in the desert's sand met their sight. The horses snuffed the refreshing smell of water, and horses and men, faint, weary, and famishing, exerting all their strength started on the full run for the blessed Eden before them, and soon sank down upon the soft green grass by the side of a clear, bubbling spring.

"Now I will leave you," said the little man. "Give me my bow and quiver. We are even, I showed you the water, and you brought me to it."

"Not quite so fast, my little friend," said Dick. "Before I give you the bow and quiver, or permit you to leave us, you must lead us to the treasure of the valley, then furnish us with a guide, two good mules, and as much of the treasure as we can carry away."

"I accede to your proposition on one condition! Never attempt to point out the treasure to any one, or to return to it yourself. If you do, death will swiftly follow, and the treasure you shall carry away will be lost to you and your family for ever.

So they gave the promise he required,

and as they were very tired they conclu-
ded to wait till morning and made their
frugal supper under the trees, drinking
plentifully of the clear, delicious water;
and slept peacefully till morning.

The little gray man woke them early.
" Come," he said. " The sun is rising, we
must away." So they arose, and taking a
drink of water and eating a tortilla, started.

For some hours they traveled on in the
pleasant morning air, and just as the sun
was beginning to be scorching in its heat
they entered a deep ravine, and there they
saw the wonderful Golden Boulder, and
countless precious stones, and nuggets of
bright yellow gold scattered round it upon
the shining sand.

Dick and his companions, were bewildered by the glittering spectacle, and a
thousand glowing visions filled their minds.
The little gray man blew a shrill whistle.

Another little gray man appeared, and bowing low, said humbly :—

" What is the will of the master ?"

" Food and drink !" answered the master.

The slave prepared a more comfortable meal than the young men had enjoyed since they left the encampment, and they ate heartily while the slave served them.

When they had eaten, the chief ordered the slave to laden the mules with treasure and conduct the young men to the confines of the valley.

Then Dick returned the bow and quiver to the gray chief, and bid him good-by.

" Never forget your promise, or beware !" said the gray man, as they turned away, and looking back they saw in the distance the last of the little man with up-raised fingers.

"He is saying again beware !" said Dick, laughing. How they went, neither of the young men could tell, but in a wonderfully short time they were out of Death's Valley. The Indian returned to his tribe, but Dick, with a happy heart, started for Fort Tejon, and after a speedy and safe journey he reached his early home.

It soon became rumored about, that he was the richest young man in the whole country. In a short time, poor Dick, the half-breed, was forgotten, but every one courted Don Richard Fielding, the rich and elegant Spanish gentleman.

There was a great feast made at the fort, when Don Richard was united in the "holy bonds of matrimony" with the Colonel's lovely daughter, and never was man more happy than he, when he led his golden-haired bride through the halls of his pleasant mansion.

"We will travel by-and-by, love," he whispered. "But first we will rest and be happy in our own dear home!"